THE MOSS O' RORA

Poems & Tales Of North East Scotland

By
Allan J.R. Thomson

Published by the Author:
Allan J.R. Thomson,
Mount Pleasant,
2 Parkhill Place,
Kirriemuir
DD8 4TA
Tel: 01575 573632

ISBN 978-0-9565007-6-2

Printed and bound by Robertson Printers, Forfar

THIS BOOK IS DEDICATED
TO MY GRANDCHILDREN

© Allan J.R. Thomson
2010

With Best Wishes

Allan J.R. Thomson

FRONT COVER - *Peat Cutters at Rora Moss circa early 1900's*
Image courtesy of Aberdeenshire Council

INTRODUCTION

I would never describe myself as a poet. I'm just a product of the land, a country lad that has got some pleasure out of writing a few verses.

I was born in Ellon, Aberdeenshire, in 1945. My parents came from Buchan crofting/farming stock. My earliest memories are of living at Hardslacks Farm, Hatton and then Slains Lodge, Cruden Bay, where my father was a ploughman.

In November, 1949, when I was four, we moved south to Broadleys Farm in Perthshire, where my father was employed as an Aberdeen Angus herdsman. I attended school in Dunning, Auchterarder and Perth. My first two years at school were not particularly happy, thanks to a somewhat old fashioned teacher who severely reprimanded me for speaking the Doric of my mother tongue, but I knew nothing else! I therefore grew up bi-lingual in terms of accents as I quickly learned to speak like my Perthshire school pals but on crossing the threshold of my own home switched easily back to my native "Buchan" and so it has been to this day. The majority of the poems are in the Buchan dialect, with the remainder being Angus and Perthshire orientated and also one from Dundee.

The production of this little book has been a labour of love and a hobby, but I am also concerned that there is a creeping Anglicisation of our Scottish culture which seems to accelerate with each passing year. As I listen to the children talking on their way to and from school. I am aware that their speech is nothing like it was a generation or two ago and I mourn the loss of old Scots words and phrases as they disappear from everyday use. If these few pages can slow down the process, even just a little, I will be satisfied.

Unlike my forebears, I did not work on the land, but had a career in the Police with Angus Constabulary, London Metropolitan Police and finally Tayside Police. My wife Evelyn and I have lived in Kirriemuir for 34 years.

Allan J.R. Thomson,
Kirriemuir, 2010

FOREWORD

I have just finished reading this excellent compilation of poems and stories by Allan J.R. Thomson and I am truly sorry that I have reached the end! I could cheerfully have read as much again.

Told in the couthy Doric, these sharply observed, yet warmly human writings present wonderful word pictures of a way of life which now, sadly, belongs in the past. But what a treasure trove for those of us who hold dear our fond and lasting memories of Buchan and its redoubtable people, and indeed, what a mine of information for following generations.

I am indeed honoured and privileged to contribute this Foreword to such a worthy collection from the pen of fellow fiddler and law enforcement officer Allan J.R. Thomson.

Sandy Ingram, O.B.E.
Glamis, March, 2010

P.S. You may, like me, find the Glossary of great assistance.

CONTENTS

Introduction iv

Foreword v

Colour Plates:

Peat casting at Rora Moss .... *after p8*

Mosside Croft .... *after p20*

Alex Ogilvie .... *after p64*

Maggie Wall .... *after p84*

John Rennie (2 pictures) .... *after p88*

Slains Castle .... *after p118*

10 Downing Street .... *after p128*

The Moss o'Rora 1

Davy 10

A Hazel Stick and The Dog 11

Winter Long Ago 12

The Factor 13

Shady Dell 14

Willie's Waiscuit 15

Black Affronted 16

My Mither's Craft 20

Witin For Siller 22

Bogie Roll 24

Dae Ye Mind 25

May 26

Aal' Ed Bruce 27

The Lang Byre 29

Dismabumlookbiginthiss 31

The Gowden Seeds o' Simmer 32

Grunny Sangster 33

Lizzie's Geets 45

Whitemoss 47

Brose 48

Alone 49

I Wonder 51

CONTENTS

Tattie Time 52

Be Prepared 53

The Saltire 55

Waaldies 56

Rotary Duck Race 57

Rotary Travelling Casino 59

Rotary Auction 61

Peter's 100th 63

Alex Ogilvie 64

The Silence 66

Norah Broon 67

A Fine Start Ti Wir Holidays 68

My First Teacher 72

Oor Wee Skail 73

Butcher Loon 74

Gordon & Joyce Webster's Farfar 75

The Quine Next Door 76

Catlaw 77

The Hairst Meen 78

Far's Ma Glesses 78

Skelpit 79

The Smiddy 80

Grunny's Broth 82

Did Ye Ivver 83

Maggie Wall 84

Hamesick 85

Tak in a Tattie 86

Summer 87

John Rennie 88

Sunday Nicht 90

Back From The Brink 91

A Winter Tragedy 93

The Minister's Two Step 97

CONTENTS

The Aal Mannies' Seat 99

Poppies 100

Grunny's Clocks 101

No Way To Treat A Lady 102

Bessie's Waall 106

Global Warming 107

Autumn 108

Tin Lizzie 109

The Drysteen Dyke 110

Winter 111

Mither Tongue 112

The Rural 113

Snares 114

Cain and Abel 116

Dinna be Coorse Tae Little Loons 117

Slains Castle 118

Rainy Tuesday 119

Green Deuk Aiggs 120

Sic Easter Sic Ear 125

The Aal Peat Stack 126

Oot O' The Shewin 127

Ten Downing Street 128

The Robin 130

The Neep 131

The Secret Land 132

Murray The Puddock 135

The Caal 136

A Country Wench 136

Seagulls Aiggs 137

The Shortest Day 138

The Turra Coo 139

Fifteen Sixty Nine 141

Feelings 142

CONTENTS

Twa Hunter Lads 143

Hippens 144

Loupie For Loup 145

Christmas Day 146

Wir Lum's Up 147

That's Naething 148

A Skein o' Geese 149

Kittlins 156

Meh Dundee Doag 158

Hogmanay 159

Another Time And Place 160

Shakkins ee' Pyoke 161

The Hens' Pot 162

Wullies Appendix 164

Rural Wifies 170

Siller Tae Buy A Coo 171

Clerkhill 172

Throwe The Bree 181

Auld Lang Syne 182

Glossary 183

THE MOSS O' RORA

".....Sax mile north o' Peterheid
There lies the Moss o' Rora.
A muckle wild an' win'y place
Wi hedder, funs an' flora....."

The great Moss of Rora lies to the north west of Peterhead and extends to about 5 square miles of flat, featureless muirland surrounded by farms and small crofts. The moss is a wild and desolate place covered in whins, heather and a wide variety of flora. Wasteland though it is, it nevertheless provided an essential and necessary element in the life of local residents. With that area of Buchan being largely devoid of trees, the surrounding communities in days gone by all got their fuel by digging peats from the moss. The banks from where the peats were cut, could be several feet deep and there often was a trench of black peaty water at the foot of them. In the winter of 1838, a great snow storm swept through the area and was still referred to many years later as the "Muckle Storm." Rora Moss was not a place to get lost in particularly during winter.

A number of crofts stood on the northern edge of the moss at that time. Among them was Bruce's Croft which consisted of a heather-thatched cottage, byre and outhouse. The croft extended to around 8 acres and although small was sufficient for a family to live on but only just. It was occupied by James Bruce, his wife Kirstan and their three children, George (Doddy) 9 years, Lizzie 6 and 3 year old John (Jecky). The land the croft stood on had originally been part of a much larger estate but after the Jacobite rebellion of 1715, the laird had his land forfeited by the Crown which eventually sold the estate to the Merchant Maiden Company. This was a consortium of Edinburgh gentlemen drawn from the Governors of the Maiden Hospital and The Company of Merchants of the City of Edinburgh which had considerable land holdings in and around Peterhead. Representatives from the

Company would travel from Edinburgh by steamer and visit their holdings periodically and report on the good husbandry or otherwise of their many tenants in the area.

Sunday, 7th. January, 1838, dawned dark and cold. It had been frost for several weeks and the ground was rock hard. A cold north wind swept over the moss making an already cold day even colder. After attending the little kirk at Kirkhill, it was usual for the Bruce family to walk over the moss to the small clachan of Rora which lay to the south of the moss. There they would have Sunday dinner with Kirstan's mother and father, Isabella and George Craig. Dod, as George was known, was the local blacksmith and had been in the smiddy at Rora since taking over from his father some fifteen years previously. The Craig family were well known and respected in the area as the smiddy had been in their possession for several generations. Indeed on a yellowing page in copperplate handwriting the Aberdeenshire Poll Book of 1696 recorded their forebears thus:-

Shire of Aberdeen. Parish of Longside Cont'd.

James Craig, Wheelvricht and Blacksmith
in the Smiddy of Rora...£2.18/6d
Elspet Mitchell,
his spoufe and son in familia ther,.........................£1.5/- 0d
Grizzel Webster, maid servant ther,......................£0 10/6d

His Poll...£4.14/-0d.

This particular Sunday, Kirstan visited her parents alone with her children. Jim Bruce had decided to stay at home as their cow had started to calve and Jim's experience of such things told him that this was likely to be a difficult birth. The Merchant Maiden Company had increased his rent the previous year despite the fact that he was in arrears to the tune of £16.15/6d. He did not like this situation.

It was due to a depression in agricultural prices and most of his neighbours were in the same boat. However, Jim Bruce existed just above subsistence level and walked an economic tightrope. A jolt whether through personal ill health, a bad season or the loss of livestock could mean the difference between survival and eviction. He could therefore ill afford to lose a calf or worse, both the calf and its mother, so he stayed at home that day.

When Kirstan arrived at the smiddy just after 1 o' clock it had already been snowing for half an hour or so. All through the meal her mother Isabella had peered anxiously out of the window keeping an eye on the weather. She had spent all of her life in the area and knew only too well what a Buchan winter could be like. "I'm nae pitten ye awa Kirsty, bit I dinna like the look o' that day," said Isabella to her daughter after they had eaten. "If the winn rises it'll be smore drift an ye'll hae a joab gettin ower the moss wi the littleens." By now it was about half past two and it was snowing steadily and had reached a depth of about 4 inches. Kirstan took her mother's advice and started to get her children ready for the two and a half mile walk back across the moss to their home.

The bairns rebelled a little as they liked to spend time at the smiddy with their grandparents. "C'mon noo, you eens," admonished Kirstan.
"Hurry up an get yer cwytes on an lat's get on i road afore i snaa gets ower deep." "Dinna forget the eerins I got for ye," said her mother handing her a small message bag. Kirstan's father, Dod Craig was asleep in his chair by the fireside. Working in the smiddy six days a week was gie hard graft and Dod liked to relax on the Sabbath. He was a big able chiel and from his build it could be seen that he was aye at hame at mait time. That Sunday, Dod had enjoyed his two helpings of broth, boiling beef with chappit tatties, a thick slice of mealie dumplin followed by rice pudding. After the meal, a comfy chair and warm peat fire ensured that he was sound asleep in no time. Isabella gave him a

nudge, "C'mon fadder, wull ye walk ower the moss a bittie wi Kirsty an the bairns seein it's snaain?"

Dod awoke with a start. "Snaain? Did ye say snaain?" "Aye," said his wife. "It's been at it iss file." "Och dinna buther dad," said Kirstan. "I'll easy manage." Kirstan was her father's daughter and was big and well built. As a teenager she had helped out in the smiddy and as a crofter's wife she was no stranger to hard work and could tackle the moss in her stride but it was the three little grandchildren that Isabella was most concerned about. "Ye could easy bide the nicht," said her mother. "Na," said Kirstan. "Jim wid juist worry aboot's. We'll be a richt, it's nae far."

Kirstan and her three children accompanied by Dod set off to cross the moss about a quarter to three. Little Jecky was carried in his mother's arms and Doddy and Lizzie held their granda's hand. The two older children were excited and happy to be walking in the moss with their granda and looked on the trek through the snow as some sort of adventure to be enjoyed. There was a stiff breeze coming from the north and it was still snowing although not too heavy. Away to the north and east, the sky was dark with the ominous threat of severe weather to come. After half an hour they had almost reached the halfway point and despite the falling snow, could just make out the twinkling lights of the small crofts on the north perimeter of the moss one of which was their home. On seeing their destination, Kirstan said to her father, "Juist you turn for hame dad, we'll be a richt noo." Dod bade his daughter and grandchildren farewell and turned for home confident that they were in no danger and would soon reach their croft.

The snow was deeper now about 6 inches or so. Kirstan strode steadily on towards their croft still carrying the sleeping Jecky in her arms. Doddy was leading the way a few yards ahead and Lizzie was walking beside her mother. Suddenly and without warning, the wind picked up and became quite strong. It was blowing directly from the north and their route home took them straight into the teeth of the gale. This wind, born of the Arctic's frozen womb came of age in a howling fury as it raced across the great Moss of Rora, its long icy fingers searching, probing and tearing. The snowflakes became much thicker and the lying snow started to drift. Visibility dropped to around 15 yards and Kirstan could hardly see Doddy up ahead of her. "Wite a meenit min," she shouted to him. "Lats mak up on ye." Doddy stopped and waited for his mother.

"Faar's Lizzie?" Doddy asked with concern when Kirstan had caught up with him. Lizzie was nowhere to be seen. Fear gripped Kirstan at that moment. She was aware that Lizzie had been walking beside her but had not noticed that she had fallen behind. The ferocity of the wind would have drowned out any cries for help. Kirstan and Doddy turned back and retraced their steps for about 60 yards where to their relief, they found Lizzie quite distressed and crying. She was stuck in deep snow having wandered off the by now indistinguishable track and had fallen down a peat bank into a drift. Kirstan comforted her and made sure Doddy and little Jecky were alright before setting off again. The increasing gale meant that the visibility was now down to about 10 yards with Kirstan and her bairns exposed and vulnerable to the wind's terrifying onslaught. In retracing her steps and stopping to attend to Lizzie, Kirstan had not noticed that the changeable wind had veered from north to easterly. Unwittingly disorientated, Kirstan set off directly into the face of the wind as before but was unaware that in doing so, this was taking her away from the direction of her home and eastwards into the centre of the moss.

The little group struggled on delving through the deep snow as darkness began to fall and tiredness and fatigue set in. By this time, the children were cold and frightened as the chill blizzard tugged remorselessly at them. After a while Kirstan realised that they should have reached their croft some time ago. She began to panic as it slowly dawned on her that they were lost. Buffeted by the wind and almost blinded by the stinging swirling snow she had no idea where she was nor which direction she should go in. The children noticed her distress and began to cry. All of them were now sodden, frozen and exhausted as Kirsten tried to get some shelter from the wind and snow in the lee of a peat bank.

> "....Ae winter's nicht lang, lang ago
> A young wife an' her bairns
> Got lost amang the wreathes o' snaa
> Fin comin hame wi eerins....."

About the same time as Kirstan left her parents' home to cross the moss, Jim Bruce was attending to his cow. It was fairly dark in the small byre and he had lit the paraffin lamp for more light. The birth of the calf was imminent but it took another hour and a half before it was safely delivered. On leaving the byre, Jim got a surprise at the ferocity of the snowstorm outside. With no light coming from the window of his little house, he knew that his wife and bairns were not yet back. He looked anxiously towards the moss in the direction that they would come but saw nothing. Concerned for their safety he put on a heavy jacket and strode off with a lantern into the moss to look for them.

> "....Her worried man gaed oot tae look
> Bit ne'er a sicht he saa'
> As far he trudged that winter's nicht
> Aye deeper got the snaa'....."

The storm raged for two days and nights before abating. Wednesday, 10th. January, 1838, dawned cold and clear. It was frosty with a blue sky and no wind. Where the snow had drifted, it reached up to the eaves of the houses. In living memory, no-one had experienced such a storm. Dod Craig and his wife Isabella had been consumed with worry about their daughter and her family but had no means of finding out if they were all right. Dod ventured forth that morning towards the moss but the snow was far too deep for him to attempt a crossing. With the wind gone, an eerie white silence engulfed the whole community. Dod looked across the moss towards the crofts on the north perimeter where his daughter's home was. He could see that in each case save one, a ribbon of peaty smoke snaked skywards. He immediately realised the significance of this and sank to his knees in the snow.

Eventually, a thaw set in and for weeks afterwards, Dod Craig, his neighbours and friends searched the moss but could find no trace of the missing family. Rumours began to circulate that they were not in the moss at all but had left the area because of the rent arrears on the croft. It was reported that they had been seen boarding a steamer in Aberdeen and were now living in America. A roup was held at Bruce's croft with the proceeds used to pay off their rent arrears. The croft was then let out to another tenant and life in the community slowly returned to normal.

Thirteen year old Craigie Slesser had left the school at Easter and had taken a fee helping the shepherd at Mains of Kininmonth farm to the north west of the moss. A broken fence had proved too much of an attraction for their flock of 80 Cheviot yowes and lambs and on Monday, 14th. May, 1838, several had strayed onto the moss. Craigie and his mongrel dog Gyp had successfully rounded up the yowes and lambs, returned them to the field and repaired the fence.
However, it became apparent that one yowe had lost her lamb and Craigie accompanied by Gyp, went back to the moss to search for the missing lamb. Back and forth they went with Gyp running out and back in large figure of eights but with little success. Although it was mid May, spotting the lamb was not an easy task because of the large number of small white patches of hard frozen snow still left over from the muckle storm. After about an hour, they had reached the middle of the moss when suddenly Gyp started to bark excitedly at something at the bottom of a peat bank. Craigie ran over then stopped in his tracks. "Oh Jesis Christ," he cried in anguish as he looked at the scene before him. Crouched at the

bottom of the peat bank half submerged in water was the body of a woman, with a toddler in her arms. Snuggled close to her on either side were the bodies of a young boy and girl. Their eyes were closed and for a fleeting second Craigie thought they were asleep. The woman appeared to be smiling. "Are ye a richt?" Craigie shouted," his mind momentarily unable to grasp what his eyes were seeing.

Then he quickly realised that she had been long dead and the "smile" was just the result of decomposition pulling the skin taut to reveal her teeth.

"....Fin springtime cam' a shepherd loon
Oot lookin' for a lamb
Cam' on three bairnies lyin' deid
Like they were sleepin' calm.

Their midder had them in her airms
An' each wis cuddlet ticht
They hadnae moved the fower o' them
Since they fell asleep that nicht....."

Craigie had lived in the area long enough to know that to come back to the exact spot where he had found the bodies may be quite difficult given the large featureless expanse of muirland.
He searched around and eventually found the broken shaft of an old peat spade which he stuck into the top of the peat bank as a marker before running back to Mains of Kininmonth to raise the alarm. A party of farm workers and crofters returned with him to the moss and recovered the bodies.

They continued their search and that same day, found the body of Jim Bruce lying face down in the peat about a quarter of a mile to the west of where his family had been found.

Peat casting at Rora Moss, Peterhead, in the early 1900's
Image courtesy of Aberdeenshire Council

> *"....Their fadder syne they cam' across*
> *Lyin' caal an' stiff an' weet.*
> *Tho' hardened were the crafter lads*
> *They a' began tae greet...."*

Dod and Isabella Craig never really recovered from losing their only daughter and her family. Isabella took things very badly and to the end of her days, blamed herself for not insisting that Kirstan and her children stayed the night with them. Dod too felt it was his fault and never forgave himself for not carrying on across the moss with them until they were safely home. Along with the help of neighbours, Dod placed a large red granite slab at the centre of the moss near where his family had died. Using his blacksmith's skills he engraved and affixed a brass plate...

> *"In memory of James Bruce, his wife Kirstan Craig and their*
> *children*
> *George, Lizzie and John who perished near this spot*
> *Sunday, 7th. January, 1838".*

George Craig outlived his wife and died aged 84 in 1872. Every Sunday for as long as he was able, George walked out to the centre of Rora Moss to stand a while at the granite slab. To this day, the path between what was the smiddy and the middle of the moss is known locally as "Doddy Craig's Road".

> *"....An' still the soughen win's blaa ower*
> *The hedder funs an' flora.*
> *It is a caal an fearsome place*
> *The muckle Moss o' Rora...."*

DAVY

Davy wis an only bairn
His midder's pride an' joy
The aipple o' his fadder's e'e
An affa' special boy.

Porritch wis nae eass for him
He got his eggs saft bilt
An' stovies nivver crossed his moo'
For Davy he wis spilt.

He didna' rin wi' idder loons
When they clim'd the grassy braes
For Davy he wis ower weel dressed
An' feart tae spile his claes.

The bairns they tried tae play wi' him
But their baa's he widna' catch
Their midders hid 'im a' wyed up
"He's jist a dampt spilt vratch."

Eence in his teens he teen a lass
That cam' oot fae Tullynessle
But Davy's midder said,"Na, na."
For Davy he wis special.

Noo Davy sits 'imsel' at nicht
His aal' folk's baith awa'
He wishes he wis young again
An' socht tae catch a ba.

A HAZEL STICK AND THE DOG

My aal hazel stick it stan's in the neuk
As stracht as the day it wis pu'd
Bit it's nae the same for me I'm afraid
For I'm aal an' ma back is gie boo'd .

I min' fine the day I cut oot that waan
Juist fifteen an new left the skweel
Wi a dog o' ma ain an fine hazel stick
I wis young an' ill tricket as weel.

Syne hame tae the hoose an raiket the shed
For ma fadder's aal carvet ram's horn
A rub wi the file an a licky o' glue
It'll a' be richt ticht gin the morn.

Noo mony's the mile I've geen wi ma stick
Ower hill throwe wuid an doon dale
It's fower dogs it's seen aff the face o' the earth
An it's been wi's at ilky sheep sale.

The dogs they're awa an ma legs are gie stiff
If walkin up hill or throwe bog
Oh affen I wish I wis fifteen again
Wi ma hazel stick an the dog.

WINTER LONG AGO

Lang caal' days that chill the been
Wi' daylicht 'oors that's hardly seen.
On ilky track there's icy slidder
It's deid o' winter a' thegidder.

˙ Snavvie bree dreeps fae the thatch
Throwe misted gless caal' bairnies watch.
Witin' for their trachled midder,
Oot for peats in clorty widder.

In win'swept parks bedraggled sheep
Hoast an' scrape at frozen neep.
Their sodden fleeces wye them doon
An' dubby rattles hing a' roon'

Syne tilly lamp or can'le licht
drags oot the lonely winter's nicht
As huddlet roon' their peaty flame
Each cottar femily sits at hame.

THE FACTOR

Factors have never been the most popular of people. The highland clearances and the disgraceful treatment and eviction of tenants are remembered even to this day. Tenants were always at the mercy of unscrupulous landowners and factors. Those tenants who diligently worked their crofts or farms often found themselves penalised for their good husbandry by having their rents increased whilst the rent of their less industrious or capable neighbours stayed the same. In many country areas the factor, being the agent of the landowner, was disliked and viewed with suspicion. Before cottages were modernised with the installation of inside toilets a common saying with many country people when they went outside to relieve themselves was, " I'm awa' oot tae pey the factor!" Such was their contempt for the man who held that position.

Sax fit three an' dressed in black
Wi' cassen e'e an' humphy back.
The factor raps wi' scra'ny hand
"There's rent tae pey." he will demand.

His jackda's een o' palest blue
Will peer an' blink at onything new.
Wi' your weell kept place he'll be content,
A gweed excuse tae raise yer rent.

But ask him tae repair a reef,
It's then that he will turn richt deef.
Throwe yalla' teeth he'll sook an' bla'
There's nae siller left for that at a'.

So 'ear on 'ear ye'll mak' an' mend,
A wife an' bairns on you depend.
Ye dread the knock o' yon scra'ny hand
For it's "Rent tae pey." he will demand.

SHADY DELL

In shady dell of mossy green
The trickling stream meanders.
Ower polished stone and fallen leaf
Its aimless journey wanders.

There summer foxgloves gently wave
A lilac hand and fingers
And hiding neath a fallen branch
A yellow primrose lingers.

Mottled sunbeams dance a jig
With leafy ferns unwound
As creeping shamrocks feel their way
To carpet wooded ground.

And brooding boulders old as time
In lichened silence sleep.
Their ancient vigil cold and grey
For centuries to keep.

WILLIE'S WAISCUIT

Willie got a waiscuit bocht
O' funcy claith an' colours
His mither brocht fae Peterheid
An' teen it till The Bullers

The Sunday skweel gaed on a trip
An' Willie he wis vaunty
He wis best dressed o' a' the loons
An' wis richt prood an jaunty

Doon tae the beach they a' did go
An' in the sea they went
Syne bigget castles on the san'
An' climm'd the heichest bent

But time for hame it seen did come
An' Willie's brain wis wracket
Tho' up an' doon he looked a' roon'
But couldna' fin' 'es jacket

A 'ear gaed bye an' simmer came
Eence mair tae sea they traivellet
Syne set for hame wi' bellies fu'
An' clyes an' hair a' raivellet

"Oh sic' a time we hid 'i day,
Bit I'll tell ye fit wis best.
I fun' ma funcy waiscuit tee,
'Twis in aneth ma vest" !

BLACK AFFRONTED

For a relatively quiet little northeast seaside town its Sheriff Court was quite busy. Not because the locals were any worse behaved than those elsewhere but there was always a number of "passing through" clients some from the nearby military base, others were itinerant agricultural workers and there were also occasionally those from boats that had docked in the harbour.

The Sheriff Court was an imposing granite building with stepped gables dating from 1872. Indeed that was the date carved on the Sheriff's large red leathered oak chair that sat behind the bench. On the ground floor were the offices of the Procurator Fiscal and Sheriff Clerk. Upstairs was the Sheriff Court itself, two witness rooms, the Sheriff's room and also two committee type rooms one of which was used for the Juvenile Court.

On the very top floor was the caretakers flat. This was the domain of Geordie Steele, a squat, pot bellied man in his sixties. As well as his caretaking duties, Geordie also acted as Court Officer and sat in on court proceedings. When required, he would go out into the corridor and shout out the names of witnesses when they were called to give evidence, his deep gruff voice resonating along the long corridor. He had been caretaker for a good number of years and as such he knew well the tattooed, unwashed, scruffy individuals who regularly appeared in the building. Wild though they may have been when they got into trouble in the town, they knew that within the court building they daren't cross swords with Geordie and their behaviour was therefore suitably subdued. Solicitors too were wary of Geordie. The regulars knew the score and watched their step but any new or visiting solicitor was in danger of incurring Geordie's wrath if he or she stepped out of line. Geordie took a great pride in the appearance of the court building and everything was spotlessly clean and polished.

In the corridor, solicitors would often stand speaking to each other or conferring with their clients. Woe betide them if they inadvertently leant against the corridor wall! "Hey min," Geordie would shout aggressively. This shout would be ignored by any solicitor unfamiliar with the building or its irascible caretaker "Hey min," Geordie would again shout but in a louder and more commanding voice. This time the culprit might look enquiringly towards Geordie incredulous that such gruff remarks could possibly be directed at them. "Aye, you!" Geordie would retort angrily. "Tak yer bluiddy sweaty han's aff ma wa'." The offending individual would then smartly stand up straight as Geordie, yellow duster in hand, wiped the wall.

Some of the more haughty legal profession did not take too kindly to Geordie's apparent disrespectful behaviour towards them and would complain to the Sheriff Clerk who merely shrugged his shoulders and would say, "Oh well, that's just George," and there the matter would end. However, it could be guaranteed that the lesson was well learned and never again would the chastened solicitor dare to lean against Geordie's wall.

Geordie was slightly deaf and this in itself could cause both embarrassment and stifled laughter within the court. Geordie often sat beside the duty constable in the court and was not slow to voice his opinion of the characters who lurked in the dock or of their sniggering pals sitting in the public benches. The problem was that due to his deafness, Geordie's stage whispers could be heard by all. No more so than in the juvenile court. This was held in a smallish committee room as it was felt that it was not appropriate to have miscreant children under sixteen appearing within the actual Sheriff Court room. Within the committee room, there was a large mahogany dining type table and along its length on one side were three high backed oak chairs. The Sheriff sat in the middle chair resplendent with black gown and wig. On his left sat the Sheriff Clerk and on his right sat the Procurator Fiscal both of whom also wore black gowns. Near the table sat the duty constable who noted the sentencing of the errant children in a large ledger. Beside the constable sat Geordie.The case would be called and Geordie would go out into the corridor and fetch in the accused child who was usually accompanied by both parents.   On being ushered in and on seeing the array of black gowns and the Sheriff's wig the young criminal would often start to snigger.   The parents on the other hand looked suitably subdued and often the mother would be sniffling into her hankie. Most times the child would plead guilty and the Fiscal would outline the facts of the case at the conclusion of which the Sheriff in his cultured tones would ask the father, "Have you anything to say about the boy?" (It was usually boys who appeared in the juvenile court). At this, the father who would often be a well built agricultural worker or lorry driver would shift uneasily from foot to foot, look down at his scrawny, plooky faced 12 year old and say, "Weel ma Lord, I juist dinna ken fit tae say. He's ower the tap o' me!" Geordie would listen to this in disbelief, look first at the small boy and then at the huge father and in a stage whisper to the constable which could be heard by all utter, "Kick e's bluiddy airse!"   There would then be stifled throat clearing and coughs from the Fiscal and Sheriff Clerk in an attempt to drown out Geordie's observations but of course they were always half a second too late!

One occasion saw a second year pupil from the academy appearing having admitted taking a knife to school whereupon he cut up several coats and jackets that had been hanging in the cloakroom. On this occasion, the Sheriff said to the boy in tones that went completely over his head, "You're a horrid nasty boy. Why do you behave so beastly?" The bewildered child stood in silence but the Sheriff's question was quickly answered by Geordie, "Kis e's juist a coorse little bugger!" Cue, coughs and throat clearing from the Fiscal and Sheriff Clerk!

On another occasion, the culprit was wheeled in followed by his father and weeping mother. The expression on the father's face said it all. He was not a happy man. The Fiscal outlined the facts telling the Sheriff that the boy had been caught stealing dinner money from his school mates. The Sheriff then asked the father if he had anything to say about the boy and the court's expectation was that as in so many cases, "He's ower the tap o' me," would be forthcoming. However, not this time. The father took a deep breath, looked the Sheriff straight in the eye and said. "Fin I heard fit he'd deen, I took him an' geed him a bluiddy gweed hidin". He continued and pointed a finger at the cowring youth, "The wife an me are juist fair black affronted tae hae tae come tae a place like iss because o' that. An' fin I get 'im oot o' here, he's gaan tae get anither bluiddy gweed hidin'." Geordie looked on open mouthed and speechless. The boy got six months probation and on leaving the room, thwacks and yells could be heard all the way down the corridor as the black affronted father taught his son a lesson. Never again did that boy come before the court.

MY MITHER'S CRAFT

My mother was born in 1921 at Mosside Croft, Hatton, Aberdeenshire. The croft, as the name suggests, stood at the edge of a muir or peat moss about 2 miles north of the village. It was a typical croft house, peat fire, no electricity, outside well and lavatory. I lived there for the first few months of my life until my parents moved to a farm nearer Cruden Bay. Mosside had been built by my mother's great grandfather on land "taken in" from the peat moss. Life was hard. My grandmother died of consumption (T.B.) aged 19 when my mother was only 2 and my mother was brought up by her grandparents, her father having previously gone to Australia to seek a new life for himself and his wife and daughter. However, the premature death of my grandmother put an end to their plans. Following the death of her grandmother in 1938, my mother and her grandfather worked the croft alone - her uncles all being away at the war. Her grandfather was a hard taskmaster. She recalls that on the morning of her wedding, he sent her to the moss for a barrow load of peats - Nae hairdresser that day then! When I am up north I often visit her old croft and just stay a while absorbing the atmosphere and silence.

Oh tae tak' the road again
Fin simmer win's are saft
An' walk the Moss o' Cruden
Far stan's ma mither's craft.

The aal' hoose noo is empty
Nae peat fire in the grate,
The windae panes are missin'
Its reef wants mony a slate.

The gairden's lang syne disappeared
There bonny flooers eence swayed
An' heather's claimed the dryin' green
Far bairns sae happy played.

Mosside Croft, Hatton of Cruden, Aberdeenshire - "My Mither's Craft"
Picture by Allan J.R.Thomson

But stannin' in this special place
There's scent o' broom an' briar,
The craft it comes tae life again
I can smell the aal' peat fire.

I see the faces that I knew
Their voices lang syne still,
Oh I could bide for ever mair
On Cruden's heather hill.

WITIN' FOR SILLER

Jeannie's aal' aunty
Wis gaa'n doon i' hill.
She said, "Aunty Maggie,
Ye should mak' oot a Will".

"Ye'r hoose an' yer siller
Should a' be wrote doon".
"Noo dinna pit aff,
So dee it richt soon."

Jeannie gaed in
At least twice a day.
Fin the La'yer cam' by,
She made 'im his tay.

Richt pleased did she hear
Fae the man in the suit,
She wis heir till a fortune
Wi' naething left oot.

Jeannie made a fuss
O' her elderly aunt.
Nae job wis ower muckle,
She nivver said "Can't."

She washed a' her dishes
Syne hoovert the fleer.
Her chores for aunt Maggie
Gaed on for ten 'ear.

Jean polished the speens
That Maggie had got.
Stumpet wi hallmarks
They'd be worth a lot.

She sat in the gweed room
An' suppet her tay.
"A' this'll be mine."
She aften wid say.

Bit month efter month
Aal' Maggie hung in
Twis Jean's only hope
That some day she'd gie in.

Ye'd think that by noo
She'd be wuntin awa'
Aal' auntie's are stubborn
Fin they tak' the thraa'

But ae winter's nicht
Aal' Maggie grew sick.
Thocht Jeannie, I doot
She'll nae lest the wik.

Twa days later,
Things cam tull a heid.
But Maggie's aye livin',
It's Jeannie that's deid!

BOGIE ROLL

Bogie Roll was the name given to a coarse, thick black, twisted tobacco supplied by an Aberdeen firm called Mitchell's. It is said that the name derived from the River Bogie in Aberdeenshire. It was very popular among pipe smoking agricultural workers. It was sold by the ounce in a rope like form about 18 inches long folded and bound in the middle with a silver wrapper.

My Granda eased tae smoke a pipe
It aye wis in 'is moo'
An affen fin I think o' him
I feel the smell o't noo.

The stem it wisna' lang ava'
The bowl it wis brunt black
My Grunny said that if he could
He'd smoke a hale peat stack

Bogie Roll wis fit he took
Nae ither kine' wid dee
He'd sook an' spit syne hoast a bit
An' the rik wid ower 'im flee

Bit him an mannies like 'im noo
Are a' gaen hine awa'
An Bogie Roll ye canna' get
Tae smoke or yet tae chaa'

Tibacca noo is nae the same
It is gie funcy stuff
It's in a tin that smells o' scint
An' isnae' worth a puff!

DAE YE MIND

As a 16 year old I moved from Perthshire to Forfar to live in digs and start my first job. Apart from 3 years spent working in London in the mid 1960's, I have spent all of my time in the area and have a great affinity with Forfar and its people. The "Andra" mentioned below refers to Andrew Smyth who was a well respected Forfar Town Councillor in the 50's, 60's and 70's. A "sic" is the Forfar word for a sixpence (2 1/2p).

Dae ye mind fin pies jist cost a sic
An' breid wis half a croon.
Fin factory bummers soonded aff
An' wakened a' the toon.

Fin Soshie shops sell't a' yer needs
Fae butcher meat tae claes.
O' sic a bra' toon Farfar wis
In thae lang faar aff days.

Message loons gaed roon' wi' bikes,
The milk cam' tae yer door.
An' blue tits howket for the cream
In days o' snavvie smore.

The young eens gaithered at The Hub
There wis nae trouble there.
Syne strolled alang tae Castle Street
For a whilie wi' Mosh Dear.

A bobby aye stood at The Cross
Tae' watch the world gae by.
Faar are they noo, thae muckle cheils
That look't efter you and I?

On Setterdays ye'd saunter roon'
Tae Keiller's up the stair.
A coffee and a hame made scone
wi' plenty jam tae spare.

The cooncillors then they did their best
For the guid o' a' the toon.
But what wid Andra' mak' o't noo
If he could look aroon'?

The faithful gaed tae Station Park
Tae cheer the boys in blue.
Then half time pies cost jist a sic.
Ye'll pey a lot mair noo!

MAY

Sweetly smells the blossomed bough
Where cuckoos cry in the misty howe.
The geese have long since left for home
And crops grow fast in fertile loam.

Whin and broom ablaze with yellow
Greet the twittering, diving swallow.
And soaring high in cloudless blue
An unseen skylark sings anew.

Distant hills in smoky haze
Hint of summer's coming days.
The stubborn snows recede at last
As springtime tells that winter's past.

Beeches flaunt their new green gowns
As nature says farewell to browns.
With higher sun and longer day
We welcome in the month of May.

AAL ED BRUCE

In the 1960's my family lived on an estate on the outskirts of Perth.   The estate shepherd was Ed Bruce.   He drove a battered old landrover and he and his dogs would be heard long before they were seen.   Ed was a rough diamond and a first class shepherd.   I often used to help him during school holidays etc.

Ed looked aaler than his years
His job wis herdin' sheep.
He looket ower three hunner yowes
Wi lambs as weel tae keep.

His hazel stick wi' iron crook
wis firmly in his han'
As he strode throwe the grassy parks
An then a while he'd stan'.

His sharp broon een wid cast aroon'
An' he wid quickly see
A yowe that hid gaen on 'er back
Or een doon on a knee.

Ed's sunbrunt face wi' withered lines
Wid crack wide wi' a smile
As he recalled some funny tale
While we walked mony a mile.

The dogs an' him they whiles fell oot
An' Ed wid shout an' sweir.
The words he used they were gie roch,
Nae fit for a lady's ear.

An' fin there wis a busy time,
I'd tak' some days aff skweel
Tae help him oot wi cuttin' tails
An' ither bits as weel.

Noo when the Laird he did appear
Ed didna' bow his heid.
"He's jist a mannie like oorsel's,
We'll a' be equal deid."

An' so he lived a busy life
In his hamely shepherd's hoose,
An' aft a smile comes ower ma face
When I think o' aal' Ed Bruce.

THE LANG BYRE

Unless they were born at home, most children born in and around Forfar and district would have first seen the light of day at the Fyfe-Jamieson Maternity Home in Taylor Street, Forfar. It was affectionately known as "The Fyfie" and also quaintly but equally affectionately as the "Lang Byre." Being in the centre of a wide agricultural area, this latter name probably stemmed from the layout of the building which was not unlike that of the many byres in farm steadings throughout Angus. The main entrance of the hospital was in the centre with two wings stretching out to the right and left of the entrance. The building was so named Fyfe-Jamieson after its benefactor, Mrs. Fyfe-Jamieson of Ruthven, Angus, who planned, built and equipped the hospital at a cost of £20,000. It opened in 1939 and at that time was one of the best in Scotland. The hospital closed after over 50 years of excellent service following maternity facilities being centralised to Ninewells Hospital in Dundee. In its heyday, new mums were very well looked after by Fyfe-Jamieson staff . The food was excellent and weather permitting, patients could sit and enjoy or walk in the extensive and well kept grounds. At that time, there was none of the production line deliveries with the 24 hour turnaround that occurs today. After giving birth, a new mum might spend 5 or more days in the Fyfie and would be completely rested before going home with her baby. On entering the hospital, you could detect an air of quiet ordered efficiency. Nurses were smartly dressed in crisp blue and white starched uniforms and the place was spotless. No superbugs lurking around in those days!

I long for simple days lang syne
When weemin a' wore frocks
And bairnies did fit they were telt
Or else got skelpit docks.

Then hospitals were a' scrubbed clean
And smell't o' soap an Dettol
And matron sternly ruled the roost
Wi nursies o' richt mettle.

The Fyfie it wis ae sic place
Whaur mony first saw licht
And Farfar mums'll fondly mind
O' that special day sae bricht.

And I did mairry a bra' sweet lass
That is ma hert's desire
Like ithers she is richtly prood
She wis born in the toon's lang byre.

DISMABUMLOOKBIGINTHISS

The few words that I dread tae hear
are said tae me affen times a year
I kid oan that I'm deef and miss
"D'ya' think ma bum looks big in thiss?"

I hate tae shop on a crowded floor
An' try an' stand richt next the door
Then sternly, she will glower an' hiss
"Di's ma' bum look big in thiss?"

"Wull a' tak the green, or d'ye like the blue?"
"I like them baith. It's up tae you"
"Well, it's either this, or maybe that,
But di's ma bum in yon look fat?"

Nae mettir fit I say is wrang
I've tell't short lees, an' some that's lang
An' I've even tried tae gie'er a kiss
But still her bum looks big in thiss

For years an' years we hiv been shoppin'
But noo it's time that I wis stoppin'
An' the question that I wunna miss
Is, "Di's ma bum look big in thiss?"

THE GOWDEN SEEDS O' SIMMER

Parks they are a' shorn an' bare
The ploo turns ower the stibbles.
Grain's teen hame tae cornyards
Noo safe fae shooery dribbles.

The rodden trees are laden doon
Reid berries a' ashimmer
An' cairriet on the win's saft airm
The gowden seeds o' simmer.

Tatties sleep in lang stracht dreels
Their sha's a' withered doon.
Syne gaithered up tae wheatstrae pits
In the lee o' each fairm toun.

An' so for winter's caal' we wite
The kye are in the byres.
Syne hame for supper weary walk
Tae cosy warm peat fires.

GRUNNY SANGSTER

For as long as anyone could remember, Grunny Sangster had lived alone in her small croft of Berrylea just north of Ellon on the Peterhead road. She kept a cow and sold home made cheese and butter to supplement her pension. Grunny was a favourite with neighbouring kids who would visit her to be read stories from her "library" of well thumbed books. This was her routine and she was happy with her lot. Little could she have known that Monday morning, 9th. June, 1958, what was later to ensue.

In late afternoon she was dozing in her rocking chair and awoke with a start, "Goad almichty, is at the time already?" she said to herself in the manner of old ladies who are accustomed to living on their own. "I'll hae tae gie masel a shak or else Mary'll be here wi ma eerins an me wi ma dennir dishes nae deen." She dozed off again and her daughter Mary entered placing a basket of groceries on the table. "C'mon mam, iss is nae eass. Sleepin 'ere like a bairn. I could've robbed the hale hoose." "Na, na." said Grunny, "I've juist iss meenit shut ma een. Did ye get ma eerins?" "Patience umman," said Mary. "Lat's get ma coat aff. Is there a sup tay in yer pot?" "Juist help yersel, an poor me een inna," said Grunny. Mary poured the tea, took a mouthful and grimaced. "Gyaad sakes, iss tay's caal! Foo lang his it been stunnin?" "Nae lang," said Grunny, "Juist since dennir time." "Bit it's five bye fower!" said Mary. "Wull I mak fresh?" "No dinna buther," said Grunny getting a little crabbit. "It's ower near tay time noo." "Ah weel at'll be at an," retorted Mary. "I'll juist dee withoot inna. In ony case, Jimmy'll seen be here. I tell't 'im ti cry in by on his road hame fae the skweel." "Oh at's fine," said Grunny softening a little. "I aye like tae see Jimmy, he likes his grunny. I'll maybe read him a story, he likes at."

Mary had started to put away the groceries when the door burst open. In bounded two laughing schoolboys of about 10 years old. "Fit like the day Grunny? Weel, Weel mam," shouted Jimmy.

"I'm richt pleased tae see ye Jimmy," said Grunny. "C'mon an gie yer aal grunny a hug." "Na, na, hugs is juist for quines," replied Jimmy somewhat coy and embarrassed in front of his pal. "Faa's iss loon ye've brocht wi ye the day?" asked Grunny. "Iss is Davy Cheyne, the shepherd's loon fae Moss End fairm. He's juist new flitted 'ere." "Far did ye bide afore ye cam ti Mossie's?" asked Grunny. "Hine awa'," replied Davy somewhat shy in strange surroundings. "Bit foo far's hine awa? Fit wis the name o' the place?" asked Grunny. "Hillheid o' Rora," said Davy. "I ken it fine," said Grunny. "Fin I wis young, I worked for the Elricks in the big hoose 'ere. Is it still Elricks that's ere?" "As far's I ken," replied Davy reluctantly. "An fit's yer fadder's name?" probed Grunny. "Charlie," said Davy. "An wis his fadder Davy Cheyne fae Backhill o' Rora?" asked Grunny. "Aye, at wis ma granda, bit he's deid and sae's ma grunny," said Davy sadly and then in an aside to Jimmy. "Dis she aye speir 'i guts oot o' abody?" "Nivver mine 'er Davy." said Mary coming to his rescue. "A grunnie's are like at." "Mine wisna," replied Davy. "Your grunny wid've been Jeannie Daveson fae Blackhulls at Peterheid," said Grunny. "Aye," replied Davy. Grunny looked thoughtful and nodded her head. "Oh aye ma loon, I fairly ken faa ye are noo."

"Wull ye read a story tull's grunny?" asked Jimmy, bringing the interrogation to an end. "Fit een wid ye like?" asked Grunny, indicating her shelf of old books. "You pick een Davy," said Jimmy. Davy examined the shelf of tattered books and selected a volume. "Treasure Island by Robert Louis Stephenson. I like iss een." He gave the book to Grunny who opened it, cleared her throat and started to read. "Eence upon a time...." She got interrupted by Davy who sounded puzzled. "Dis she nae need glesses?" "I nivver use em." retorted Grunny. She resumed. "Eence upon a time there wis a pirate ca'd Lang John Silver..." Davy interrupted again, "At's nae fit's on i first page." He looked over her shoulder and read out loud. "It says, Squire Trelawney, Doctor Livesy and the rest of the gentlemen asked me to write down the whole particulars about Treasure Island."

Grunny resumed her reading somewhat flustered. "Oh aye, wite a meenty. Far wis I? Aye, Squire Trelawney, Doctor Livesey and the gentlemen asked me to write doon aboot Treasure Island." She struggled. "Eh, Lang John Silver wis een o' the pirates...." Davy interrupted impatiently, "At's nae richt. Read fit it says." Grunny resumed but had hardly started when Davy in exasperation shouted. "Ye've geen wrang again!" Grunny closed the book and lowered her head. "Ye canna read, can ye nae?" asked Davy quietly. With head still bowed Grunny confessed softly. "No laddie, I canna read." "Aye she can, she can read better nur onybody," shouted Jimmy protectively. "She's read a' thae books tae me hunners o' times. Hiven't ye Grunny?" "No Jimmy, Davy's richt." said Grunny quietly. "I canna read. Fin I telt ye stories I wis juist makkin things up." Jimmy started to cry and gave Grunny a hug.

"C'mon you loons, awa ootside an play a filie," said Mary. The boys went out. Mary was alone with her mother and took hold of her hand. "C'mon noo mam, fit's iss nonsense aboot you nae being able tae read? Is ir something wrang wi yer een? Is it glesses ye need?" asked Mary sympathetically. "No Mary, glesses wid be nae eass," said Grunny. "Ye see, I nivver learnt tae read." She sobbed gently. "Fin I wis little, I juist gaed tae the skweel till I wis seven syne ma midder took nae weel wi consumption an deet. I hid tae bide at hame tae help ma fadder wi the craft. I suppose it wis aginst the laa nae gaan back tee skweel bit naebody buthert muckle at at time. There wis lots o' bairns helpin oot at hame." Mary interrupted. "Bit fin I wis little, ye read a the books tae me an for ears ye've been readin them tae Jimmy."

"Weel," replied Grunny, "I juist made it a up. The books belanged ti ma fadder. He liked tae read an fin I wis little, he read ti ma ilky nicht so I kint maist o' the stories aff bi hert an the bits that I forgot I juist made up. You nivver jaloused and neither did peer little Jimmy." "Bit foo did ye manage fin ye hid forms tae full up an a that?" asked Mary. "At didna happen affa affen," said Grunny. "Bit fin it did, I got Toam Kelman the postie tae full em up for ma. I juist tell't im I'd broken ma glesses. He wid show ma far tae sign ma name. I can write ma name, bit at's a.

"Oh mither, fit a shock," said Mary recovering slightly. "Bit listen, it's nae the en o' the world. It'll nae mak ony difference tae us. Ye can still tell Jimmy stories if ye'r that gweed at makkin them up. Bit if ye've ony forms tae full up, forget aboot at ull fashioned breet o' a postie, I'll dee them for ye."

"Oh Mary, fit a relief tae get that aff ma shooders," sighs Grunny. "I wis aye feart tae say onything in case ye thocht ill o's." "Dinna be silly," said Mary in an attempt to lighten things up. She laughed and said, "Noo than mam, is there ony mair skeletons hidin in yer press that we should ken aboot?" Grunny hung her head, hesitated then replied falteringly. "Aye Mary, there is." Mary slumped into a chair. "Oh mam, fit neist?" she cried. Grunny started to weep and blurted out. "Ye hiv a brither Mary. His name's Sandy an he bides in Canada." Mary's face was ashen. She stood up and angrily demanded. "Oh for goad sake mither, fit on earth's been gaan on?" She burst into tears. "Fan did iss happen? Faa else kens? She slumped down at the table . "I dinna even ken ma ain mither, the shame o't, oh me."

Grunny regained some of her composure and started to speak slowly and deliberately. "Mary, as I tell't ye lang ago, ye nivver kent yer dad." She indicated a yellowing portrait photo of a kilted Gordon Highlander hanging over the mantlepiece. "Kis he wis killed in the Great War. Fin you wis born, it wis twins that I hid, you an a little loonie. I wis in service at the big hoose at Hillheid o' Rora at i time. Kennen that your dad had been killed, the Elricks said they wid help me oot an keep me on for a file bit said that I could only keep een o' ma bairns, so I hid tae gie een o' ye awa. I juist didna ken fit tae dee. Syne ma brither fae Stonehaven got in touch we'se an little Sandy went tae him an es wife. Ye see, she couldna hae femily so Sandy wis brocht up as their ain." Grunny reminisced, "Oh he wis a rare little loonie, fair heidit wi a little pug nose juist like yer dad's."

Mary rose from her chair, dried her eyes and embraced her mother. "Oh mam, fit a hard life ye've hid. Bit foo did ye nae tell's a this ears ago? Did ye nae keep in touch wi Sandy?" "Weel, at at time ye juist did fit ye wis telt," explained Grunny. "I wis gled tae hae a reef ower ma heid, bit aal Elrick wis gie strict an sent for the minister an they baith telt ma fit I hid tae dee or else I wid be putten oot." She resumed thoughtfully. "Aye, I've hid mony a sair greet late at nicht fin I hid time tae think aboot it a."

"Oh mam, fit wye were they sae coorse tull ye?" asked Mary. "It wis ower the heid o' yer dad an me nae being mairriet," answered Grunny. Mary cupped her face in her hands in shock, " I nivver kent at! Oh me." Grunny continued. "We hid planned tae get mairriet bit yer dad got called up ti the war an wis sent awa afore we got roon tull't. Syne I discovered I wis expectin. At at time, it wis gie hard for ye if ye had a bairn an wisnae mairriet so I juist kept quate an worked awa at the big hoose. I moved on efter a ear an abody thocht I wis a war weeda wi a young quine so I nivver made them ony the wiser. There wis a lot o' young weemin on their own wi young bairns juist efter the war so naebody thocht onything aboot it."

"Bit did ye nivver hae ony uptak wi yer brither an Sandy?" asked Mary. "No neen ava," said Grunny. "Ye see, Sandy thocht that ma brither an his wife were his real mam an dad so there wis nae uptak. But syne they hid a faa oot. Sandy wis telt the richt story fin he wis aboot twenty an there wis a row. Sandy thocht that they should've telt him fa he wis richt fae the start. Onywye, Sandy emigrated tae Canada efter at."

"Bit did he nivver come tae see ye," asked Mary. "Dis he keep in touch?" "He cam ti see ma juist eence," replied Grunny. It wis in 1935, juist afore he gaed ti Canada. He wis a big strappin chiel, fair heidet wi a little turned up nose, juist like yer dad." She smiles wistfully at the recollection. "We baith hid a richt gweed greet. I've a lump in ma throat iv noo juist thinkin aboot it. He said that he wid write tulls bit I tell't im I couldna read so he juist laached an said that I should say my glesses wis lost an get somebody tae read for ma." "An did he write?" asked Mary excitedly. "Faar's es letters? Faa read them tull ye?" "He's nae muckle o' a letter writer," said Grunny. "It's been twenty three ear an I've only gotten fower letters. I nivver asked onybody tae read them in case a the goins on lang ago cam oot." "Bit is he a richt, fit div the letters say?" asked Mary anxiously. "Oh, I dinna ken fit they say," said Grunny. "I juist taks them oot an looks at them an touches them files. Kennen that he'd touched them as weel made me feel closer tull im. He must be a richt kis I juist got the last een twathree wiks ago." She reached to the shelf beside her chair and handed Mary a shoe box. "They're a in ere." Mary removed the lid and brought out four blue envelopes tied together by a red ribbon. Mary untied the ribbon and opened the first letter. "Oh me, ma hands are shakkin," She started to read.

"Berrylea Farm,
Tribune,
Saskatchewan,
May, 18th. 1939....."

Grunny interrupted excitedly, "Div ye hear at Mary. He's named his place efter iss craft."
Mary resumes.

" Dear Mother,
        At last I have got round to writing to you. It's been
4 years since I arrived here and a lot has happened. I did a few
odd jobs at first and then along with a party of other Scots, I

moved to Saskatchewan. The Canadian Government were awarding parcels of land to those who had worked on farms. I applied and got a place near Tribune. It is in wheat country and I have 1,500 acres..."

Grunny sounding incredulous gasped, "Fit did e say? Fifteen hunner acres? Goad almichty!"

Mary continued. *"My nearest neighbours are five miles away. They helped me build my house and barn. I got married to a Canadian girl called Laura three years ago and we have a little son, Alexander, who is two years old and we have another on the way. I see the news from Europe is not good. It looks like there could be another war.*

Hope you are well.
Your loving son,
Sandy.."

"Weel I nivver." said Grunny. "Funcy that, my ain little loon a grown up wi a big fairm an femily in Canada. It maks ma richt prood". She reached for her hanky and started to sniffle. "Aye mam, he's deen a richt for imsel." said Mary. "Go on Mary, said Grunny impatiently, "Read i next een tulls." Mary did as she was bidden.

"Berrylea Farm
Tribune
Saskatchewan

April, 10th. 1946.

Dear Mother,
        It is a while since I wrote........."
"Aye iss't." interrupted Grunny, "Seyven ear!" "Ye maybe canna read bit er's naething wrang wi yer coontin," responded Mary.

" Oh get on wee't," said Grunny impatiently.

Mary resumed.

"It is a while since I wrote but we are all fine. Alexander is 9 and goes to school in Tribune, he is in the 4th. grade. Holly, our little girl is in the 2nd. grade. We are keeping our head above water on the farm but only just. The wheat prices have not been good these last few years and everyone is struggling but I'm sure good times are just around the corner. With the war over things may start to improve. I didn't have to fight as I got an exemption through working on the land because food production was very important.

Hope you are o.k.
Your loving son,
Sandy."

"He mith hae lattens ken afore noo he didnae hae tae fecht," said Grunny in faked annoyance. "I worried aboot im a throwe the war! Go on Mary, read i neist een."

Mary continued.

"Berrylea Farm,
  Tribune,
  Saskatchewan.

January 18th. 1958.

Dear Mother,
  How fast the time flies. I hope you are well. We are in the middle of a severe winter, it is often 30 degrees below outside. These last few years have been better and we have prospered some. As well as growing around 1,000 acres of wheat I have 80 head of beef cattle as well. Alexander is 20 and helps on the farm. Holly is 18 and will leave home to start university in the

fall. The best news of all I have saved for last. With Alexander helping on the farm, I am able to sit back so have decided to come home to see you..."

Grunny rose from her chair excitedly, "Div ye hear at Mary, he's comin hame! he's comin hame! At last I'll hae ma ain loon at ma ain fireside." She claps her hands with glee.

Mary continued reading.

"I have everything arranged and arrive in London on the evening of 8.6.58. I'm booked on the overnight sleeper to Edinburgh and I'll be in Aberdeen just before 3 p.m. the next day so should be joining you for tea that evening.

Your loving son,
Sandy."

"Hey mam, at's i day, he'll be here i day!" shouted Mary excitedly. "Na, nae the day surely," said Grunny unbelievingly. "Aye he wull, I'm tellin ye," said Mary. "Look, i letter says he's in London on 8.6.58. At wis yesterday..." "I'm nae eass wi dates." interrupted Grunny. "He'll hae arrived in Aiberdeen iss efterneen at 3 o' clock," said Mary. He'll come aff Burnett's half past fower bus tae the Broch." "I've naething for es tay!" said Grunny sounding worried. "Nivver min aboot es tay iv noo. He'll seen be here," said Mary. She looked out the small gable end window. "Here's Burnett's bus comin doon i lang stracht, it'll seen be at the ain o' the road!" "Is it stoppin Mary?" asked Grunny anxiously. "Aye iss't," cried Mary. "Oh me, has he cam aff Mary?" asked Grunny, "Div ye see im?" "Somebody's cam aff, bit it's nae him," said Mary disappointedly. "No, it's juist a young quine." "She'll likely be makkin for the big hoose," answered Grunny. He must've missed the bus or the train. Bit are ye sure aboot the dates Mary?" Mary picked up the letter and read out loud. *"I have everything arranged and arrive in London on the evening of*

8.6.58. So I'm richt eneuch wi the date. Iss is Monday the 9th. o' June."

Grunny rocks in her chair, "Ach, he'll likely be here the morn. Efter twenty three ear anither day'll nae mak nae difference." "Oh bit wite a meenit," said Mary thoughtfully. "Lat ma see at letter again. She repeats, "*I arrive in London on the evening of 8.6.58.* Ye ken fit I think mam? I think he's nae comin till the 6th. o' Aagust. Dis the Americans an Canadians nae write their dates roon the wrang wye? Div they nae write i month first an syne the day?
If at's the case it'll be the 6th. o' Aagust afore he's here."

Mary sat down at the table and the two women had a good laugh. She then noticed another blue envelope lying there. "Oh mam, I hinna read the last letter, the een ye got some wiks ago." Mary examined the letter closely, "It's fae Canada richt eneuch, bit it's nae fae Sandy, the writin's different." She opens the letter and starts to read.

"Berrylea Farm,
Tribune,
Saskatchewan.

Dear Mother,
                I am your daughter-in-law Laura, I write to bring you some bad news. Your son Sandy, my dear husband is dead..." "Oh no, surely no," cries Grunny rising up. Mary breaks down but continues, *"We had a real bad storm at the end of February and Sandy got caught up in it and perished. I'm sorry to bring you such bad news. Please forgive me for not writing more but I am too upset.*

Your loving daughter-in-law,

Laura."

"I canna believe iss," sobs Grunny.   Mary puts her arm around her mother and tries to comfort her, "I dinna ken fit tae say, it's sic a shock."

Just then the door opens and in comes Jimmy and Davy followed by a tall fair haired girl of about 18 years.   Jimmy points to Grunny sitting in her chair and says to the visitor, "At's her sitten ower ere." The young girl approaches the rocking chair and takes Granny's hand in both of hers.   She kneels down so that they are both at eye level.   Her soft Canadian voice trembles with emotion, "Granny, I am your grandaughter Holly Sangster from Kennada".   Grunny rises from her chair and embraces Holly. Mary joins in as well.   Jimmy and Davy look on in disbelief as the three women hug, cry and laugh all at the same time.
"Oh lassie, I'm richt pleased tae see ye," says Grunny.   She indicates to Mary, "Iss is yer auntie Mary, yer dad's twin sister." Holly goes on to explain that as her dad's trip to Scotland was all booked and paid for she just paid a few dollars to get his name replaced by hers on the travel documents and decided to come in his place before she went away to university.
The women chatter excitedly until Mary becomes aware of the two boys looking on in astonished bewilderment.   "C'mon you twa loons," she admonishes. "Dinna stan ere wi yer moos open like ye wis catchin fleas. "Say hello tae Holly.   It's nae ilky day ye get tae meet a freen fae Canada."   She indicates Jimmy to Holly and says, "Iss is my loon Jimmy, an iss is his pal Davy Cheyne fae up i road." Holly shakes both boys' hands, "I'm very pleased to meet you," she says, "Jimmy, I guess you and I will be cousins."

Mary looks at Davy and feels a little sorry for him, "Michty Davy, you'll be winnerin fit's gaan on an feelin rale oot o't, you bein the only ootsider amon a us Sangsters." "Aye a wee bittie," says Davy shyly.   Grunny came to his rescue, "Na Na Mary, Davy's nae an ootsider.   He's een o' us.   If I'd gotten mairriet tae yer dad, my mairriet name wid've been Cheyne.   Yer dad an Davy's granfadder were brithers.   So in the hinnerain, we're a Cheynes, ilky een o's." "Oh Grunny," cries Davy, he runs across and embraces her.

Holly stays with Grunny for two weeks before returning to Canada. Several weeks pass and Grunny resumes her routine. It is a warm afternoon and Grunny is dozing in her chair. The door opens and in comes Tom Kelman the postman. "Weel mistress Sangster, fit like the day?" asks Tom. "Nae sae bad Toam. Ye're later the day are ye?" says Grunny.   "Aye," says Tom, "Ma bluiddy aal bike got a burst tyre gaan up the moss brae so I took a filie tae get it sorted.   I see the Moss End lads are in amon their hairst." "Aye," says Grunny. "Aal Mossie aye likes tae be first whether it's ready or no.   Help yersel tae yer tay Toam, it's nae lang made."

 Tom does as he is bidden   "Foo did ye get on wi yer visitor yesterday?" asks Tom.   "Visitor?" asks Grunny, "Fitna visitor? There wis naebody here estreen."   "Goad almichty umman, I spoke tull im masel." "Far aboot?" asks Grunny.   "At the fit o' the road," said Tom. " He wis comin up fae the turnpike aff the half past fower bus. He speirt if Grunny Sangster still bade at Berrylea. I tell't im that I had juist hid my fly cup fae ye, so he held on up i road."

"Fit did he look like?" asked Grunny. "A smert chiel, taal wi fair hair an a turned up nose," said Tom. Grunny sank into her chair, "Oh me. Fit wis yesterday's date?"

"Wednesday," said Tom. "The sixth o' Aagust!"

LIZZIE'S GEETS

Illegitimacy is not just a modern trend.   It will have happened at all levels of society through the years.   It was certainly common in the country areas of Scotland and in particular among those who entered domestic service.

Oh Lizzie wis a sonsie lass
An' held in high esteem,
An' she did rin the muckle hoose
The Laird's ain kitchie deem.

Tho' mony lads had coorted Liz
There's neen socht her tae wed,
Bit affen in a meenlicht nicht
They'd come an' share 'er bed.

Lizzie cooket for the Laird
An' washed an' cleaned 'is beets.
She worket hard fae morn tae nicht
So's she could raise her geets.

Ilky een looked clean an' snod
They got on weel thegither
Fin sittin' at the Sunday skweel
Were a credit tae their mither.

But 'ears pass by an' bairns grow up
An' each must mak' a start
Tae venture doon life's road fae hame
Tho' it brak's a mither's heart.

Sandy he wis first tae leave
A handsome strappin' chiel.
The tears they welled in Lizzie's een
An' in the Laird's as weel.

Fa' his Da' wis neen did ken
An' Lizzie widna' tell,
But mony whispered roon' aboot
That it wis the Laird 'imsel'.

Jimmy syne he flew the nest
For sooth he took a train.
He jined the Gordons wi his pals
An' fell at Alamein.

Then Maggie cam' tae tak' the road,
She moved tae Hilly's fairm.
It wisna' affa' lang ava
Till young Hilly took 'er airm.

Mary she wis gweed wi' books
An' she bade on at skweel.
She did become a teacher lass
A job she did richt weel.

The youngest o' them a' wis Jean
She bade at hame wi' Mam,
Looket efter her in her aal' age
Until her time it cam'.

Young Lizzie wis an only bairn
An' Jean she wis her mither.
Her father wis the blacksmith's loon
Or it micht hae been anither.

Oh Lizzie wis a sonsie lass
An' held in high esteem,
An' she did rin the muckle hoose
The young Laird's kitchie deem.

WHITEMOSS

The Whitemoss is the name given to a wood and marshy loch between Aberuthven and Dunning in Perthshire.

Still and deep your waters lie
Where yellow reeds surround
A boggy marsh to guard against
Intruders to your ground.

Mallard ducks they paddle by
Their rasping cries still calling
As lonely coots chirp in the reeds
With evening shadows falling.

A dredging swan with graceful neck
In silence sweeps the shingle
As swooping swallows sip a drink
where dancing insects mingle.

And in the failing evening light
The blue sky fades to red
As shoals of starlings twist as one
And none can know who led.

BROSE

In years gone by, oatmeal formed a staple part of the diet of many country people in Scotland. It would be taken at least once per day in the form of porridge, oat cakes, skirlie, white puddings or brose. Brose was particularly popular with the single men on farms, particularly those who had to do their own cooking because it was simple to prepare and could be made in a matter of minutes. Several table spoonfuls of medium oatmeal were put in a bowl, salt to taste then add boiling water and stir vigorously with the handle of the tablespoon. Add full creamy milk and you had a meal fit for a king. Care had to be taken however when adding the water as too little meant that the brose was stiff and unpalatable and too much would "drown" the brose.

The girnal's fu' o' fine new meal
Aa' pressed doon tae keep it weel.
There's mealie jimmies we can mak'
Or corters o' breid wi' cheese tae tak'.

Bit porritch maistly starts oor day
An' sen's the bairnies on their way.
File grumpy granda blaa's 'es nose
As 'e sits 'ee neuk tae steer 'is brose.

It's five big speens o' meal 'e tak's
Syne wi' saa't 'es nae neen lax.
An' the watter his tae be weel b'ilt
Or else he'll girn, "Ma brose is sp'ilt."

Roon' an' roon 'e steers the speen.
The bowl's jist like a sharpenin' steen.
His words at bra'kfist time are few,
I'm sure his speen wid cut yer moo'.

Syne 'e sups wi' fine rich cream
An pechs an' slurps till its a' deen.
Tae the fireside cheer he'll then depart
An' sittin' doon will rift an' fart.

48

ALONE

Family life has always had its difficulties but none more so than at present when many families experience break-ups and separation. It is difficult for all concerned - abused wives, fathers' who are denied access to their children and grandparents who through no fault of their own have no contact with the estranged members of their family. The next two poems are written from a parent and grandparent's perspective. However, it is the children of broken homes who are the real victims._

I never saw your little face
Nor held your tiny hand
The pain and hurt of losing you
No one will understand.

I never heard your happy laugh
Or dried your childish tear
To lose a child and have no say
Was very hard to bear.

Years passed by and time went on
And you grew up I know
And often I would think of you
And oh I missed you so.

Then one day a letter came
It said that you were fine
Married with a little son
First grand child of my line.

When nervously at last we met
I looked into your face
I held your hand and heard your voice
And felt your warm embrace.

And gradually I got to know
The daughter I had lost
We got on well or so it seemed
But now I pay the cost.

For once again I am alone
No visit, phone or letter
Am I a disappointment dear
Did you hope for someone better?

Still life goes on in this strange world
I think of you each day
Of precious hours that we did spend
Which none can take away.

I WONDER

I wonder what you look like now
Now that you are four.
I wonder if they're proud of you
I'm sure they are and more.

I wonder is your hair still blond
Are your bonny eyes still blue.
I wonder if you think of me
I often think of you.

I wonder if some day we'll walk
The hills of this fair land.
I wonder if I'll tell you things
And if you'll understand.

I wonder if you'll know of me
And what you will be told.
I wonder if you'll speak to me
Before I grow too old.

TATTIE TIME

Nowadays, the potato crop is harvested by machines but in years gone by farmers placed a heavy reliance on child labour and itinerant workers to gather in the potatoes. Schools would close at the beginning of October for what was then called the "tattie holidays." The work could be hard but rewarding and at the end of the holidays each child would be taken into town to spend their "tattie money" on new school clothes for the coming winter. At a time when agricultural wages were quite modest, the earnings of school age boys and girls helped out quite a bit.

The tattie time is here again
We'll work for siller on claes tae spen'
On Setterday we'll be scrubbed clean
Then intee toon tae buy new sheen.

Tackety beets for the dubby track
Forgotten noo's wir gie sair back
A corduroy jacket wi' matchin' briks
We'll a look smert for wiks an' wiks.

Seemits, sarks an' worsit draars
Keep in the heat an' oot the haars
Wi' waaldies for the weetest days
A lang thick coat completes oor claes.

For winter days we're noo rigged oot
Oor siller spent on fine new cloot
The caal dark days they seen will pass
Then hungry kye ging oot tae grass

When simmer days are come again
We'll hope there's still some poun's tae spen'
On briks that's short an' sandal sheen
Michty, faar's the winter geen.

52

BE PREPARED

Vic and Allan were two laddies that grew up on neighbouring farms in Perthshire.   They were the same age and had started at the local village school together.   Weekends and summer evenings would see them out together exploring the nearby woods or climbing the hills.

They joined the local Cub Pack and were part of a good natured but mischievous group of young boys who enjoyed growing up in an idyllic part of the Perthshire countryside.   The Cubs met after school on a Wednesday under the watchful eyes of "Akala" - Mrs. Lawson a matronly lady and "Baloo" - Mrs. Laing.   Neither of these two women had any children and both put a great deal of effort into looking after their adopted "family" of cubs.   Each meeting was eagerly looked forward to by the boys and as time passed there was some rivalry as to who would have the most proficiency badges such as stamp collecting, knot tying, compass reading, and so on.

Now it came about that the boys were to be tested for their firelighting badge.   This entailed them being split into pairs and given two matches.   They then had to collect some dry twigs, build and light the fire and then cook a "twist."   This was some flour mixed with water into a dough, rolled into a long sausage shape then wound round a stick and cooked on the open fire. Being close pals, Vic and Allan were paired up for the test. However it had been raining heavily for about three days before the test and Allan voiced his concern to Vic that they might not get the fire to light and they would fail the test which was due to take place the next afternoon.   Vic told him not to worry as he had a plan!

After school, the cubs all met up and walked about half a mile out of the village and turned into an old track that led to a farm.   On the left hand side of the track was an area of small trees and rhododendron bushes where the tests were to take place and on the opposite side of the track was an old ruined lodge. The boys were duly split up into their pairs and went off in search of twigs. The rain had stopped by this time but the ground and any twigs lying around were all sodden. Whilst others were searching for twigs, Vic slipped unseen into the old lodge and came out with a bundle of twigs. He confided to Allan that he had collected them the day before and steeped them in paraffin overnight!

Pair by pair set down their twigs and attempts were made to get the sticks to light. Pair after pair tried and each time there was just a phhhuuussst as match after match failed to ignite the damp twigs. Then it was Vic and Allan's turn. Vic gave Allan a knowing wink and dropped a lighted match onto their pile of twigs. There was a hiss then a roar as a column of bright orange flame leaped six feet into the air singing Vic's eyebrows and making the startled onlookers leap back in amazement. The shiny green leaves of overhead rhododendron bushes soon began to crackle and turn brown.

Vic and Allan's fire was so spectacularly successful that it was an embarrassment to them and all they could do was roll about laughing. When the fire had died down a bit the two of them mixed their dough amid suppressed giggles, cooked their twist and were awarded their badges. And what of Akala and Baloo? Well they had watched all of the proceedings in stunned disbelief and never uttered a word. Perhaps the Cub and Scout motto of "Be Prepared" had been uppermost in their minds!

THE SALTIRE

Following the local authority elections in May, 2007, the S.N.P. administration in Angus lost power to an alliance of Conservatives, Labour, Liberal Democrats and Independents. The new "Rainbow Alliance" decided that they would no longer fly the Saltire flag from council buildings. This provoked outrage among the inhabitants of Angus and the new council was forced to retain the Saltire in an embarrassing climb down. To save face however, they decided that in addition to the Saltire they would also fly a newly designed flag to promote Angus. However, again to the Council's embarrassment some wag climbed the flag pole in Kirriemuir and stole the new flag but left the saltire flying!

In ancient Angus loyal and true
Auld Scotland's flag aince proudly flew.
But cooncillors come and cooncillors go
An' besoms new their power maun show.

Wi' votes a' coonted an' in the bag
Their feeble minds turned tae oor flag.
"We run the Cooncil, there's noo nae doot,
So we'll see the back o' yon blue cloot."

The cooncillors sat in pious cluster
And designed a flag- a yella' duster!
But Angus fowk o' sterner stuff
Put struttin' cooncillors in a huff.

"Touch wir flag ye spineless deils
An' ye'll feel the wrath o' Angus chiels."
The Cooncil's back wis tae the wa'
"Ach we'll dae them yet, we'll jist flee twa'."

But Angus fowk will no' be fooled
By the bigsy gowks ower which we're ruled
At election time their votes will sag
For we'll a' mind aboot wir flag!

WAALDIES

Wellington boots are known by many names. "Wellies" throughout most of Scotland, "Gum Boots" to the posh and "Toppers" to fisher folk in Peterhead. In rural Buchan, wellingtons were known as "Waaldies". Now this type of footwear was very necessary for tramping through snow or slush in wet weather and particularly so on farms where mud and puddles could be the order of the day. Whilst an essential element of footwear, they had their disadvantages, feet would sweat profusely particularly during hot wet weather. If worn for a prolonged period of time they left their "trade mark" in the form of a narrow red ring round the calf of the wearer caused by the top rim of the wellingtons flapping against the wearer's leg!

Ye needed them on rainy days
or wintry days wi' sleet,
Bit if ye wore them for a month
They sweated a' yer feet.

Noo waaldies wis a handy thing
For muckin' oot a byre,
An' fin ye took them aff at nicht
Yer feet could be on fire.

Bit hiv ye seen a pair o' socks
That in waaldies hid been worn
They jist aboot craa'lt ower the fleer
They widna' dee the morn.!

On Setterdays the quines dressed up
An' wi' funcy sheen looked slick.
Bit the reid ring gave the game awa'
They'd worn waaldies a' the wik!

ROTARY DUCK RACE

I have been a member of Kirriemuir Rotary Club for about 10 years. The Club gets involved in various fund raising events for local and international charities. These include an annual duck race at Easter in Kirrie Den. We also have a team who travel to neighbouring Rotary Clubs to provide a "Casino" and also from time to time we run auction sales to raise some funds. The next three poems take a light hearted look at these events.

The duck race day has come again
An' fowk a' flock tae Kirrie Den
"Spend twa pound and try yer luck,
An' buy a little plastic duck."

There's Farfar lehds wi' picnic behgs
Come up tae roll their Easter eggs
An' Hilltoon bairns - ye hear their crehs
"Ma', ye forgoat tae bring the pehs."

So we wore tabards o' shockin' green
Tae mak' richt shair that we wis seen
Or the colour micht hae been bricht yelly
But they widnae fit roon' Donald's belly

An' Strathie wisnae far ahent
The straps gaed ping each time he bent
Whilst the rest o' us did quietly snigger
We tell't them weel they need much bigger!

The bairns they liket James's hat
"Mither come an' look at that."
But in the burn it's ca'ld an' chilly
A soakin' there can shrink yer taes!

At the finishin' line oor lads were there
The winnin' deuks they did declare
If aince or twice they got it wrang
It's a' for fun, so what the hang!

So wi' a' the cash that we hae got
There's some puir fowk we'll help a lot
Whether near or far it disnae matter
Because o' us they'll hae clean watter.

ROTARY TRAVELLING CASINO

Casino nicht has come aince mair
An' the gambling' team taks tae the flair.
Wi' plastic pyokes a' filled wi' chips
"Noo place yer bets" comes fae their lips.
White is fine, or there's even blue
But we'll no' tak' red for an hour or two.

In his evenin' suit and lookin' swank
Sits Linsday Broon wha' runs the Bank.
When things are busy, his broo he'll dicht
But Allan's there tae keep him richt.
They're fu' o' patter wi' lots o' waffle
As they dish oot tickets for the raffle.

For them that likes tae play a hand
There's tables three whaur they can stand.
Fae big Will M. some chips they'll tak
Syne dae the same fae wee Bill Mac.
But wi' maister Duncan they'll no tarry,
They'll rue the day they bet wi' Sparry.

At chuck-a-luck they throw the dice.
A genteel game that is quite nice.
For spinster ladies fu' o' grace,
Wha's hands have never held an ace
Or folk that likes tae win some tricks
Fae lads that canna' coont past six.

There's aulder wifies wi' hair rinsed blue.
I've seen them foamin' at the moo'
Ower the 20p that they hae won
And planning' how tae hae some fun.
Their laughs and skirls will lest for weeks.
I'm shair that some hae pee'd their breeks.

The croupiers faces red do glow
When lassies young their assets show
As they bend ower the roulette table
And oor lads wish that they were able.
But few o' us still hae the means
An' as for ithers, it's in their dreams.

But all too soon the nicht has passed.
The cairds are dealt the dice are cast.
There'll be ither times tae try yer luck
We tell the punters as we load the truck.
A happy nicht wi' wir new found chums,
They're a' impressed wi' the lads fae Thrums.

ROTARY AUCTION

Tae raise some cash for puir fowks' needs,
We wracked oor brains an' scratched wir heids.
There's attics fu' o' things oot there
That we could sell, o' that I'm shair.
So we collected lots o' stuff
Tae fill the hall there wis enough.

T.V. sets an' china dugs,
Exercise bikes and tiger rugs.
An' fae a lad wha's name wis Heath,
A full set o' his granny's teeth.
Gairden howes an' bits for cars,
A gold fish bowl an' pair o' draa'rs.

A coat stand wi' a fancy peg.
An' a broon shoe wi' a widden leg.
Cardboard boxes wi' sing'le socks,
A gless e'e in a velvet box.
A black bag fu' o' lots o' claes,
Suspender belts an' ootsize stayes.

Books o' poems through which we mused.
An' a tam cat's litter, (hardly used!).
Then fae a mither, a bed tae keep
In which her loon wis still asleep!
A chastity belt a husband trusted,
Wha's mortice lock the ludger busted.

A jiner's box wi' rusty tools,
Lochgelly straps thrown oot fae schools.
A rabbit hutch an' chicken coop,
A teapot wi' a cracket stroop.
Some pickled ingans in a jar
Wha's sell by date wis oot by far

Pandrops tae sook when in the Church.
A bride a lad left in the lurch.
A bothy kist brocht in a car,
Wi' a hale week's porritch in the draa'r.
A leather splyochan wi' buttoned tags,
That held a machine for rollin' fags.

A fower tae'd graip wi' han'le slack
An' a thing tae claw an itchy back.
Strings o, beads an' wally dugs,
Twa teddy bears baith wantin' lugs.
And in an auld green canvas bag
We f'und the stolen Cooncil flag!

Noo a' this stuff that I hiv tellt
went tae the hall an' maist wis sellt,
But whit wis left wis really useless.
An' I hiv tae say that we were ruthless.
So come the end o' oor braw roup,
The lave got flung intae the coup!

PETER'S 100TH

Peter Giles is a long standing member of Kirriemuir Rotary Club
and for a number of years produced the Bulletin of Club activities
and projects.   He recently published his 100th. edition.

Wis there e'er a man like Peter Giles
Wha's Bulletins come in different styles.
There's some that's short an' ithers lang
But neen o' them ging aff the fang.

There's Rotary facts an' photographs
An' twa'r three jokes tae gie us laughs.
Wi' dates o' things we hiv tae mind
Denners, dances an' sic like kind.

His computer skills are affy slick
For his Bulletin it comes oot quick.
It tells o' fowk that wull get treats
Even afore the Cooncil meets!

But Peter, we are a' richt gled
O' the 'oors ye've spent oot o' yer bed.
Scratchin' yer heid for things tae say.
When the Bulletin's here it mak's oor day.

Yours is the best that we have seen,
You deserve a telegram fae the Queen.
She'll say tae Peter, "Richt weell done,
One's pleased tae see ye've reached yer ton."!

Wis there e'er a man like Peter Giles
There micht hae been, but I doot it whiles.
His Bulletin days they are noo past
But were richt guid whilst they did last.

ALEX OGILVIE

Alec Ogilvie was a retired Angus farmer and honorary member of
Kirriemuir Rotary Club.   Alec was an authority on Robert Burns
and was well known throughout Angus and beyond.   He was
much in demand at Burns Suppers in the area and was a regular
guest at Kirriemuir Rotary Club Burns Suppers where his
renditions of Tam o' Shanter and Holy Willie's Prayer were
legendary.   Alec died in 2006 aged 95.

Oh Eck, auld Eck, we miss ye sair
In years gaen bye ye'd tak' the flair
An' we lach'ed until wir sides were sair
Wi' tales o' Shanter.
Oh how we miss yer couthy ways
An' freendly banter.

Jist like oor Bard ye tilled the land
An' tae feel again yer calloused hand
We'd walk the length o' this fair land
Tae see yer weel kent face.
But you dear Eck are far fae here
An' restin' in a gentler place.

But is there somewhere up on high
A nicht like this in Heaven's clear sky
Whaur wi' sangs an' la'chter time slips bye
Wi freen's we knew?
Oh! sic a time they'll hae this nicht
because o' you.

The Late Alex Ogilvie in full flow at Kirriemuir Rotary Burns Supper
Picture courtesy of Bill Martin, Rotary Club of Kirriemuir

The Bard himsel' he will be there
But noo wi' Eck o' whit a pair
Airm in airm they'll walk the flair
An' dance an' diddle.
An' pausin' whiles wi' lang lost freen's
Like Paddy Liddle.

Oh Eck, auld Eck we miss ye sair
We'll hear yer hamely voice nae mair
But we're grateful that yer time did share
Wi' us fowk here.
An' for oorsel's, I hope were spared
Anither year.

THE SILENCE

Anyone who has ever owned a dog and become attached to it will know of the pain felt when the dog dies.   There are some who liken it to a family bereavement.   I don't know if I would go as far as that but it certainly is a difficult time.   Arriving home takes a bit of getting used to when instead of an exuberant welcome when the door is opened, there is just an all engulfing silence.

C'mon aal dog, noo far's yer lead
It's time tae shak yer sleepy heid.
Rax yer legs syne hae a claa,
We maun gyang oot e'en tho' it's snaa.

For ten lang years we were thegither
The best o' freen's wi een anither.
Throwe wuid or muir I'd walk wi' pride
My faithful' freen' aye at ma side.

Ye nivver eence did lat me doon
Tho' sulket if I gaed tee toon
But arrivin' hame I'd reach the door
An' hear yer cla's on linoed floor.

Syne fit a welcome I would get
Tho' it's been years, I min' o't yet
Swishin' tail an saft broon een
Pleased tae see a lang lost freen'.

But syne I noticed you were thin
Something gaed wrang gie far within.
Vets nor prayers were ony eass
You slipped awa' and are at peace.

Noo I'm at hame an' left masel
On oor happy times I aft do dwell
But there's times I greet tho' I'm a man
It's the silence that I canna' stan'.

NORAH BROON

Within Scotland there are many regional accents covering the length and breadth of the country. Indeed within counties, accents can vary between towns that are only a few miles apart. In Edinburgh there is the posh "Morningside" way of speaking whilst in Glasgow, "Kelvingrove" would be the equivalent. All of which makes the production of a Scots/English dictionary well nigh impossible. The speech of the landed gentry is different again and is upper crust English. There are those from ordinary backgrounds who would try and emulate the gentry by pretending to be something they are not. These people fool no one when they speak with affected accents. They are the subject of fun by their peers and are often described as speaking "panloaf" or "with a bool in their mooth"

A quine that I ken she spiks panloaf
Bit the words fae her moo lat her doon
Her vowels ye see, get a' mixed up
They're flat fin they should hae been roon.

She looks doon her nose at her aal school pals
The eens that she's kent a' her life
"I canna tak up wi them noo ye ken
For I'm the Provost's new wife".

She tries tae impress wi her style o' dress
Bit her skirt it is ower short o' cloot
"The hem's ower high", says she wi a sigh
"An it fair garrs ma airse stick oot".

She swanks aboot wi her heid in the air
Tae impress folk that's new ti' the toon
Faa's 'at they speir, bit it's seen made clear
That's naebody. It's juist Norah Broon.

A FINE START TI WIR HOLIDAYS

Efter sic a lang time, I doot if there's onybody left noo that min's aboot the time that the 0803 express train fae Glesca' ti' Aiberdeen cam' ti' sic a sudden hult jist sooth o' Forfar on 'i first Setterday o' the Glesca' Fair in 1951. If onybody dis mine o' that day, I'll bet they dinna ken foo the trainie cam' ti sic a hurriet stop.

Weell, it wis a' ower the heid o' a tin o' black blake, a baggie o' bruised corn an' a little quine's flannel knickers. I wis sax 'at 'at time an' I min' o't as if it hid jist happened 'estreen.

It a' started back in 1949. I wis fower 'ear aal' an bade wi' ma fadder an' midder an little sister - she wis twa', on a fairm nae far fae Slains Castle at Cruden Bay. Ma fadder drove a pair o' Clydesdale horse an' there wis anither lad worket 'ere as weel, I think his name wis Jimmie. The grieve on the fairm wis ca'd Geordie. He wis ma grunny's brither an' ma fadder's uncle an wis a gie crabbit kin' o' a lad. The fairm belanged ti' Sutherlands, the larry lads fae Peterheid.

Onywye, ae day I wis oot playin' in 'i closs an' wis busy makin' san' pies in a heap o' san' that hid been teemt in a neuk. Ma fadder an' Jimmie were in 'i byre an' there wis a gie lot o' lachin' an' skirlin comin fae their direction, bit I wis ower muckle teen up wi' ma san' pies ti pey ony attintion. Efter a file, ma fadder cam' oot an' said, "Rin roon' till yer midder an' speir at 'er ti gie ye 'i black blake an' bring't back tulls."

I did fit I wis tell't an' fun' ma' midder at 'i side o' the hoose claiken wi Geordie. "Dad's in 'i byre wi' Jimmie an' they're needin' 'i black blake." I still min' that I got a richt soor faced glower fae Geordie, an' ma mam jist ignored me. So I jist, tugget at 'er overall an' speirt for the blake again. 'Iss happened twa three times an each time I wis ignored an' Geordie's looks aye got angrier an' angrier. Seein' that ma midder wisna' gan' ti' budge, I jist gid intee hoose an' helpet masel' ti the black blake fae the box faar wi kept 'i stuff ti clean yer sheen. Back I gaed ti the byre an' sa' that as weel as ma fadder an' Jimmie, een o' Geordie's dothers wis in i' byre as weel. Jimmie had a gie ticht hud o' 'er an' she wis wrigglin' aboot, lachin' an' gigglin' an' geein' oot a skirl ilky noo an' again. I gave the blake ti ma dad an' he opened i' tin syne started ti clort 'i quine's legs wi' the blake a' the wye fae 'er feet richt up till 'er briks.

I wis ower little ti ken fit wis gaan' on, bit 'i quine wis fair enjoyin' 'ersel' an' I hid jist seen ma first blackenin' as Geordie's dother wis seen tae be gettin' mairriet. Weell, 'at should've been 'at but I dinna' think Geordie wis ower sair' pleased aboot 'i goin's on, an' fae fit I wis tell't later, I think he gaed in o' the huff. Noo, it wisna' a gweed idea ti' anger Geordie. I aye min' he eence teen an ill wull at een o' the fairm cats. There wis new hatched chuckins gaan' missin' an Geordie blamed ae parteeclar cat. Foo he picket 'iss cat I dinna ken, but ae day he took 'i double barreller an' shot 'i cat. Syne he laid it oot on a barra' an' cut open its belly. I aye min' seeing 'i chuckins' little yalla' legs in 'i cat's stammack and Geordie sayin', "See, I tell't ye 'at wis 'i bugger 'it wis aiten 'i chuckins." I dinna ken fit 'e wid've deen if he hidna' fun' 'i chuckin legs inside 'i cat! Onywye, Geordie, bein' 'is usual thraa'n sel' hid teen 'i tig ower 'i heid o' the blackenin' an' things wis gie sair made atween him an' ma fadder. Wiks passed by an' 'ere wis nae sign o' a thaa'. It didna' maitter that ma grunny wis Geordie's sister, in fact 'at mith hae made things waur. Noo, Geordie's wife an' ma midder each kept a pucklie hens an' each got supplied free o' charge wi' bruised corn ti' feed 'i hennies. Ah weell, oor bruised corn hid rin oot an' ma fadder speirt at Geordie for mair. Bit contermasheous deil that he wis, Geordie wis still in 'i deid thraa' an' tell't ma fadder, "There's nae neen, ye'll jist hae ti' dee withoot!" A day or twa' efter 'at, Geordie hid ti ging awa' somewye an' ma fadder hid a rake aboot an' cam' on 'i bruised corn hidden awa' in a locket shed. Noo, ma fadder wis a quiate, easy gaan' kin' o' a chiel, bit he hid a gie short fuse an' widna' lat onybody tak' 'im for a feel. So needless tae say, fin Geordie cam' back, the pair o' them fell oot an' ma fadder hid 'is birse up an' jist tell't Geordie faar 'e could stick 'es job.

Ma midder wis gie sair teen up aboot 'iss. Here she wis, wi' twa little eens, 'er man oot o' a job an' they hid ti get oot o' the hoose at the en' o' the wik! Weell, we left Cruden Bay, an' we ended up bidin' in a little craft caa'd Tassets Hill atween Hatton an' Ellon an' it wid be fae there that ma fadder started lookin' for anidder job. Ae day he wisna' at hame so I speirt at mam, "Faar's dad 'i day?" She said, "He'se geen hine awa'." Noo, I'd nae idea foo far "hine awa' " wis. I aye thocht that Auchiries wis hine awa' fae Cruden Bay. At least it seemed hine awa fin ye wis a little loon an' ye hid ti' waa'k 'ere ti catch the Aiberdeen bus. Bit bi the wye ma midder wis spikken, 'iss "hine awa' " wis faarer nur Auchiries!

So it turned oot that ma dad had gotten a job gie far sooth on a fairm in Perthsire as an Aiberdeen Angus herdsman at £5 a wik in 'i simmer an' £5.10/- a wik in 'i winter. We flitted in November, 1949, an' I aye min' it wis a big green cattle float that cam' ti tak us an' a' wir stuff. We even hid a new hen hoose ti tak' wi's made bi ma midder's cousin, Wullie Rennie, the jiner fae the Toll o' Birness. It wis a gie lang road sooth an' it wis dark afore wi' got ti wir new fairm. We were a' gie tired bit ma midder wis richt pleased kis she hid gotten a spleet new hoose wi three bedrooms an' an inside laavie wi a bath. The hoose hid electric licht as weel, so wir aal' Tilley lumps got 'i go bye.

We seen settled in an' come April, 1950, I wis five so I started at 'i village skweel. Noo, 'at wis a gie strange experience for a little loon a' the wye fae Buchan. Naebody kint fit I wis spikken aboot. They a' thocht that I couldna' spik richt. Fit a chik - an' me hid been spikken a' ma life since I wis twa! Ah weell, 'i neist 'ear, 1951, we wid ging hame for wir holidays an bide wi' ma grunny at Tillybrex, Birness. Ma midder's uncle an' 'unty, Johnny an' Annie Duncan fae Aiberdeen hid been doon biden wi's for a file afore they were ti emigrate ti Toronto an' they cam' back wi's on 'i train. It wis 'i start o' the Glesca' fair an' 'i train wis gie busy fin it stoppet at Perth. There wis sax o' us lookin' for seats, ma midder an' fadder, me an' ma little sister, Hazel - she wis three, an' Johnny an' Annie. We were gie lucky ti get a teem compartment a' ti wirsel's on 'i last coach afore 'i guard's van.

Me an' Hazel wis gie excited. 'Iss wis 'i first time we hid been on a train. Oor midder wis a bit on edge an' a' kis she hid hid ti cope wi' visitors and get's a' ready for wir holidays. We hidna' been gaan' lang, maybe half an 'oor oot o' Perth fin I noticed a weet bit on 'i fleer. " Hye mam, Hazel's piddlet 'ersel'." I cliped. Sure eneuch, Hazel hid hid an "accident." "Dinna' worry yersel', Nell." Johnny said ti ma midder. "I'll jist ging an' gie the weet briks a sweel oot in 'i laavie." Fin he cam' back, we winnert foo we could get 'i briks dry. "Ach, I'll jist hud on till 'em an' hing 'em oot at 'i windae," said Johnny. So 'at's fit he did. Weell, they were nearly dry fin a' at eence 'i train's brakes slammed on an' Johnny nearly gaed a' 'es lingth. The train cam' till a gie quick stop an' a wee file efter, 'i guard burst intae wir compartment, "Fit 'i hell are ye deein' fleein' a reid flag oot o' 'i windae for min?" he said ti Johnny. "Flag?" said Johnny, Fit flag? I'm jist dryin' 'i little quine's briks." an' wi' that, he showed 'i guard Hazel's bricht reid flannel knickers. "Damn 'i bit." said 'i guard. "Wir driver thocht it wis my reid flag an jamm't on 'es brakes."

"Oh me," said ma midder bursten' intae tears, "'Iss is a fine start ti wir holidays!"

MY FIRST TEACHER

My first school was in Perthshire. I started Primary 1 in August, 1950 as a gie scared five year old. There were no nurseries or play schools in those days and living on a farm 3 miles from the village I knew no one. Having moved down from Aberdeenshire with my family the previous November term, I still had my Buchan accent and so I was a bit of a foreigner and the target of fun amongst these "sooth loons and quines." My teacher, was a targer of the first order and had me completely terrified. I remember that it was never explained to me that in my sum book an "X" meant that the sum was wrong and a tick meant the sum was right. I naively thought that my sums were right and the teacher was pleased with my efforts because most of them had "kisses." After all, that was what my granny put on my birthday and Christmas cards! As far as the teacher was concerned, if your folks had a shop or your Dad was a businessman you were alright but as the son of a mere farm worker I was just grist to her cruel mill. I often wished that I would meet her in later life but that didn't happen. Maybe just as well!

A surly tyke she wis an' thrawin
When I at skweel did start,
I'd never met the like afore
It scared a wee loon's heart.

Her wattery een wid pick ye oot
Tho' ye tried hard tae hide,
Then cruelly she wid ca' ye doon
And at ye she wid chide.

Were ye no' the thickest loon
That she had ever had.
Oh how I wished that she wid come
An' say that tae my Dad.

Mental sums they were the worst
I lived in mortal dread,
An' the answer that I often gave
Wis the first thing in my head.

Of my sum book I wis richt prood
An' showed my mither this,
For ilky sum on ilky page
Wis market wi' a "kiss."

But mither's smile it disappeared
I think she felt gie sick,
For page an' page for ever more
There ne'er wis ony "tick."

Then gently she did hug me close
An' ca'd me her ain dear.
She said that she wis prood o' me
And shed a silent tear.

OOR WEE SKAIL

I have no idea who the author of the following verse is but it was
chanted frequently in the playground of our primary school.

Oor wee skail's a braw wee skail
It's made wi' stick an plester.
The only thing that's wrang wi' it
Is the baldy heidet maister.

Anonymous.

BUTCHER LOON

Before the days of supermarkets when towns and villages had a
number of independent grocers and butchers, message boys were
a common sight after school as they cheerfully went their rounds
on their "message bikes." These specially adapted bicycles had
quite a small front wheel to accommodate a large wicker basket
which held all the "messages." Each cycle also had a large
oblong metal plate fixed to the bar advertising the shop and its
wares. Message boys got a wage but often the tips on a good
round would exceed the wage.   At that time when a message
boy's job fell vacant there usually was no shortage of applicants to
fill the post.

The butcher loon has gotten a bike
An' he scoots a' through the toon.
His basket's fu' o' pun's o' mince
Tae deliver on his roon'

He is a gie important lad
The hoosewifes think he's gran'
They smile an' thank him for their beef
An' pit shillin's in his han'.

Sometimes he gets an' aipple reid
Or some toffee stiff tae chaa'.
The butcher loon's a lucky loon
Wi' the best job o' them a'.

But eence I'm bigger I'll get his bike
Syne I'll speed roon' 'i toon
Oh richt weell aff I then will be
For I'll be "Butcher Loon."

GORDON & JOYCE WEBSTER'S FARFAR

Farfar's sic a special place
It's there we've spent oor days
Wi' honest, kind an' hamely folk
In that toon 'neath Bummie's braes.

The steeple o' the auld East Kirk
Stan's guard ower a' the toon
An' welcomes hame each weary lass
Or hamesick Farfar loon.

In evenings ower the Rosie Road
We'd wander airm in airm
And dance until the wee sma' 'oors
At Achterfarfar fairm.

In winter time when nichts were cauld
We'd cuddle in the Gaffey
Or upstairs in the Regal
And then tae Moshe's cafe.

A bridie fae McLaren's
Wi' a Saddler's cake sae sweet
An' a Sky Blue win at Station Park
Made Setterday a treat.

So through life's long and twisted road
We've made oor way thegither
Happy at wir ain fireside
Best freen's tae een anither.

Vistana is oor special place
It is oor happy home
Wi' views o' Catlaw and Strathmore
we have nae need tae roam

An' tho' we've traivelled near and far
North, sooth, east an' west
The road back hame tae Farfar
Is the een we like the best.

THE QUINE NEXT DOOR

The quine that bides next door tae us
Has gotten affa fat.
Her mither says it's sweeties
Bit I'm sure it's mair nur 'at.

Her frocks they dinna' fit nae mair,
Each een is unco ticht.
Fin she boos doon tae tie 'er pints,
Oh fit a bluiddy sicht.

I hear 'er cowks each mornin'
fin she's walkin' tae the mull.
I winn'er fit 'er dad'll say
Aboot 'er visit fae a bull!

CATLAW

Catlaw and its attendant hills, Crandart and the Lang Goat lie at the foot of the Angus Grampians and dominate Strathmore. They are seen from Craig Rossie near Auchterarder in the south west and far up into the Mearns in the north east. The hills overlook the wee red town of Kirriemuir where there is a saying - "If ye can see the tap o' Catla', its gan' tae rain'. If ye canna' see the tap then it is rainin'!"

Catlaw lies amid Strathmore,
Guards east to west and North Sea shore.
With Crandart and its Lang Goat freen'
From far and near their braes are seen.

There's grouse among the heather lies
In August days of clear blue skies.
As sweating beaters scour the hill
And guns blast forth in search of kill.

But when Catlaw's brow has dust of snow
Then the summer days are long ago.
And bairns take to the tattie dreels
With old and young and tinker chiels.

Then high up in the Catlaw brae
An ermined stoat seeks out his prey.
But unconcerned the white hare lopes
Across the gentle snow clad slopes.

Proud ptarmigan with feathered feet
ower snowy ground they run to meet.
As the wintry sun sinks in the west,
A snow clad Catlaw looks its best.

THE HAIRST MEEN

Dewy mornin's caal' but bricht
Corn in stooks a welcome sicht.
Tattie dreels wi' withered sha'
Backlan' hills that wite for sna'.

Clad in silver up abeen
A silent smilin' roon hairst meen.
Doon she looks fae starry sky
An' lichts the parks as she glides by.

Wakenin' up tae clear caal air
We upward look but she's still there.
Her silver face noo washen clean
Oor silent, smilin' roon hairst meen

.FAR'S MA GLESSES

In copin' wi' life's ups an' doons
It's highs an' lows an stresses
Ilky day I loss ma rag
Fin I canna fin' ma glesses

I had them jist a meenit ago
Fin I wis tryin' tae read
An' half an 'oor o' lookin'
gets them sittin' on ma heid!

I doot I doot I'm gettin' aal'
Forgettin' names an' places
It's time I signed ma Will I think
Noo far aboot's ma glesses.

SKELPIT

In 2008, there was a lady provost on Angus Council. A female opposition councillor lodged a complaint with the Standards Commissioner for Scotland accusing the provost of assault when she allegedly smacked the councillor's bottom. Apparently the provost was waiting to start a council meeting when the female councillor turned up somewhat late but insisted on having a drink of water before the meeting commenced. After investigation, the Standards Commissioner dismissed the complaint against the provost ruling that the "smack" had been nothing more than a playful gesture.

The Provost she wis in a state
"We're a Cooncillor short, we will be late."
Syne Glennis ran in wi' hasty clatter
"Hing oan a meenit, I need some watter."

"C'mon, ye're late, ye tardy wench."
"It's time I wis sat on the bench."
But Glennis took her time tae sup
An' the Provost's birss wis really up.

"She disnae ken wi' wha' she's messin'."
"I'll teach the lazy quine a lesson."
The Provost fumed, her looks were glum
As she skelpit Glennis on the bum.

"Ouch! That wis sair," puir Glennis wailed
"It's against the law tae hae me flailed."
She looked aroond for a marble stool
Syne plunket doon her doup tae cool.

The Provost rubbed her hands wi' glee
"Noo tak' a lesson and no' cross me."
But Glennis strode oot tae the loabby
"I think I'm gaen' tae tell a boabby."

Och lassies, come on, screw the nut
Yer brains it seems are in yer butt
Much better ye'll hae tae dae I doot
Or at votin' time ye'll baith be oot!

THE SMIDDY

When we lived on a farm in Buchan, my father drove a pair of
Clydesdale horses and I can just remember being taken to the
smiddy once or twice when one of his horses had to be shod.
Smiddy's were gie fascinating places for little loons and Smiths
were men of character. Our Smith liked pandrops and kept them
loose in his pocket. He would often offer me one from his grimy
gnarled hands and I quickly learned to "sook" and spit before
enjoying the sweetie!

Doon the road fae Wattermill
A smiddy steed lang seen,
An' Clydesdale horse fae roon' aboot
Gaed there tae get new sheen.

The smith he wis a strappin' chiel
Tam Birnie wis his name.
His prowess as a blacksmith
wis kent gie far fae hame.

Tam wis fourth o' his lang line
That chappet reid het steel,
His muscles swalled an ran wi sweat
On this able Buchan chiel.

For ilky horse that cam' his wye
Tam kent it like a brither.
He could recite its pedigree,
He'd aften shod its mither.

The anvil in his reekie den
Rang oot wi' steady clangs,
As ilky shee wis hemmert flat
An' held in place wi' tyangs.

The bellas soughed at reid het cwyles
An' they did spit oot sparks.
An' Tam an' his apprentice loon
Were soaken' tae their sarks.

But horses they have disappeared
Nae mair they haul the ploo'.
An' the smiddy's noo a craft shop
Sellin' dishes fite an' blue.

An' Tam he lies nae far awa'
Aneth a granite steen.
An' Heaven's horses prood will be,
For Tam still mak's their sheen.

GRUNNY'S BROTH

Grunny she had big soup plates
O' willow patterned blue
An' muckle silver hanl't speens
Ower wide for a wee loon's moo'.

Her broth pot hottered on the fire
Wi dumplins in a cloot
A daad o' bilin beef forbye
That ye couldna dee withoot.

Carrots, neeps an' Marra' pise
Pearl barley and an' ingan
Cookin' in 'er muckle pot
In nae time it wis singin'.

At twal' o' clock fin a' wis loused
An' seated roon' 'er table,
Aal grunny took 'er muckle pot
Syne set tee wi' the ladle.

Wi a tattie placed in ilky plate
We suppet wi' a wull
An' ne'er a wird did ony spik
Until wir wimes were full

Syne yoket ti the bilin' beef
Wi dumplin's made o' meal
An' a clart o' fine het mustard
For every country chiel

Neist there cam' a plate o' rice
Wi a speen o' last 'ear's jam
Syne sleepit soun' for half an 'oor
Till een o' clock hid cam'.

DID YE IVVER

Did ye ivver sook a soorock
Fin you wis young an' feel.
Did ye ivver taste a tattie
Juist new dug fae a dreel.

Did ye ivver ate a fine wild rasp
Juicy, sweet an' gweed.
Did ye ivver feast on goossers
Yalla, green or reid.

Did ye ivver clim' the granite heughs
Tae gaither seagulls eggs.
Did ye ivver pu' the sa'ty dilse
An' ging hame wi scratchet legs.

Did ye ivver raid a bummers byke
Tae steal their cames o' honey.
Did ye ivver rip yer new skweel briks
Fin mam wis short o' money.

Did ye ivver rub a docken leaf
Far a nettle stung yer han'.
Did ye ivver wish that youth wis ower
An' you could be a man.

Did ye ivver think fin you wis young
That days wid lest for ivver
Div ye ivver long for them again
But ken ye'll see them nivver.

MAGGIE WALL

During the 16th. and 17th. centuries, over 4,000 women were executed for witchcraft in Scotland. In the 1950's, I went to primary school in Dunning, Perthshire, and before I could ride a bike, had to walk the 3 miles or so along the B8062 Auchterarder road to reach Broadleys Farm where we lived. About a mile out of Dunning on the lands of Meadow Bank Farm stands a large stone cairn topped with a stone cross. Painted white on the stone are the words *"Maggie Wall burnt here as a witch 1657"*. Unfortunately, there are no records surviving to tell us anything more about Maggie Wall. The strange thing is that the painted words are always in pristine condition and no-one ever sees anybody refreshing them. Also, in the summer time there are always wild flowers placed on the cairn but again, nobody ever sees who places them there! The monument stands close to the north side of the road in a field that usually had pigs roaming free in it. Now, imagine me as a five year old walking home alone on a dark windy winter afternoon and having to pass a witch's monument and just as you pass, an unseen pig gives a grunt or a squeal - at least I hoped it was a pig!

Near Kelty wuid there stan's a cairn
Its stanes built high an' even.
It marks the burnin' o' a witch
In sixteen fifty seeven.

Maggie Wall was the wuman's name
But there's little mair we ken
O' the dreadfu' things that she did dae
accused by frichtened men.

But a' aroon' ken o' her noo
Three hunder years an' mair,
But naething o' the cowardly knaves
That brunt the lassie sair.

Yet efter a' that lang lang time
An unseen han' appears,
An' places flooers on Maggies's grave
An' has daen through the years.

Monument to Maggie Wall near Dunning, Perthshire.
Picture by Allan J.R. Thomson

HAMESICK

Fifteen 'ear aal' an' kens the world
Wi' a new job far fae hame.
He canna' wite tae get awa'
Tho' he's bashfu' jist the same.

Syne boorded oot in ludgins strange
He's young withoot a care
But thinks lang o' his mither's hearth
An' wishes he wis there.

But Friday nicht it comes at last
An' he can pack his case
Syne sets for hame wi' lichtsome hert
Tae see his mither's face.

There's neen he'll tell fits in his mind
Tho' he kens that she will guess.
A hamesick loon's nae ill tae spot
Fin he gets a mither's kiss.

TAK IN A TATTIE

Scottish people have always prided themselves in the hospitality shown to visitors. In centuries past when the only mode of travel across country was on horseback or foot it was not uncommon for a traveller to knock on a cottage door and be given food and shelter for the night. Nowadays people have never been so well fed with a huge variety of relatively inexpensive food to choose from with exotic dishes from India, China and the Far East readily available. It was not always so. In country areas not too long ago the staple diet was meal and potatoes. At that time a lot of oats were grown to make oatmeal and used for porridge, brose, skirlie, mealie puddings, mealie dumplings etc. Plain ordinary cooking was the order of the day in country areas. In northeast Scotland it was common for folk to put a potato or two into their plate of soup. Whether it was broth, lentil or pea soup it didn't matter. When the soup was served there would also be a large dish of potatoes placed in the centre of the table and family members eating at dinner time would all help themselves to a tattie with their soup. If there was an unexpected guest or visitor sharing the meal with the family, the host would invariably tell them, "Tak' in a tattie." which was a signal that the guest was welcome and that the hospitality was gladly given.

Steamin' bickers fu' o broth
Syne herrin' that are sa'ty
Ye're welcome at oor table heid
C'mon, tak' in a tattie.

Oor fare is plain but plenty
Sit doon an' hae a chattie
Help yersel' tae hame made broth
An' syne tak' in a tattie.

The bilin' beef's a bitty scarce
An' some o' it is fatty
But a mealie dumplin's in the dish
So tak' in anidder tattie.

SUMMER

Wafted by the soft warm breeze,
Barley sways in dark green seas.
And shaded 'neath a leafy bower
A shepherd takes his mid day hour.

Down in the meadow far away
Country folk are making hay.
And standing in a running brook
A sculptured heron casts a look.

On upland muir mid grasses tall
Lapwings chase a black capped gull.
Then glinting in the fading sky
a rising trout takes casted fly.

And as the evening shadows fall
We hear the lonely curlew's call.
The sun has set but still it's clear
In northern climes mid summer's here.

JOHN RENNIE

John Rennie was my maternal grandfather. He was born in 1894 and grew up on his parents' croft of Berrylea, Aldie, in the Parish of Cruden, Aberdeenshire. He was a corporal in the Gordon Highlanders, fought in the first world war and spent time as a prisoner of war in Germany. On his return to Scotland he married and had a daughter, Helen Rennie, my mother. John emigrated to Australia in 1923 and landed at Freemantle from where he travelled east into the wheatbelt. He obtained 1,500 acres of bush land at Jilbadji location 119 in Westonia which he cleared and eventually made into a wheat farm. John named his farm Berrylea after his father's place and it was located at the south end of Carrabin South Road, Western Australia. His plan was that he would send for his wife and daughter once he had established himself but unfortunately, before that could happen his wife died of T.B. My mother remained in Scotland and was brought up by her grandparents. John Rennie never re-married and never got back to Scotland. He died there in 1950 aged 55. He is buried in plot 355 of the Presbyterian section of Bruce Rock Cemetery, Western Australia.

Neath ochred red Australian soil
John Rennie rests from earthly toil
No headstone marks the spot he lies
Nor passers by with family ties.

No flowers are laid with tender care
For none who pass know who is there
They know not of his years of life
And less still of his dear loved wife.

Long long ago ower Cruden's moss
Hand in hand they'd walk across
And plan the life that they would share
So deep in love without a care.

The author at John Rennie's grave, plot 355, Bruce Rock, Western Australia.
Picture by Evelyn C. Thomson

Site of John Rennie's Farm, Berrylea, Carrabin South Road, Western Australia.
Picture by Allan J.R. Thomson

Then married with a daughter dear
A new life beckoned far from here
So for Australia John set sail
To claim new land he would prevail.

Then later when through work and toil
He'd cleared the land and ploughed the soil
For his wife and daughter he would send
And a life together they would spend

But death it came and took a life
And John did lose his dear loved wife
Left all alone in that far land
He came to terms with fate's cruel hand

Now after long and arduous years
Through life's long road of hopes and fears
John Rennie rests from earthly toil
Neath ochred red Australian soil.

SUNDAY NICHT

The first two years at primary school were not a pleasant experience for me.   Even now I can remember Sunday nights dreading the arrival of Monday morning when I would have to get up and face school.   I remember one Christmas holidays I was out sledging with my pals on the Sunday before school started and I thought that if I just kept on eating snow I would be ill and off school.   Sure enough, the next day I was ill - I had whooping cough!   I think I was off for about three weeks but I doubt if eating snow had anything to do with it!

It's Sunday nicht an' I'm forlorn,
I dread the thocht o' skweel the morn.
Yon wifie wi' her crabbit look
Wull tutt an' pech at my sum book.

Ma writin' tee it wunna please.
I wull be shakkin' at the knees,
As terrified I leave ma seat,
I darna' lat her see me greet.

At dennir time there's nae escape.
Her angry een at me wull gape
As throwe the cowks I'll try an' ate
While she scowls at ma half teem plate.

Bit that's the morn, it's anither day
An' I hiv still ma bath tae hae.
Syne riggit oot wi' clyes that's clean,
Aneth ma vest new Thermagene.

On comes the werrliss wi' a click,
It's Michael Myles an' "Take Your Pick".
But a' ower seen the words are said,
"C'mon ma lad, it's time for bed."

It's Sunday nicht an' I'm forlorn,
I dread the thocht o' skweel the morn!

BACK FROM THE BRINK

For 24 years I was a member of the Angus Constabulary/Tayside Police Mountain Rescue team. During that time the Team was involved in numerous searches and rescues throughout the Region. Some had happy endings, others did not. This poem is a true story about a couple who got lost in the Glen Doll area of Angus in the early 1990's.

Black velvet darkness. Weightless and snug, sleeping sound. Faint ringing. Far, far away in some deep and   distant place. Louder now, then louder still. The alarm? Time to rise from sleep and face another day? No, the ringing's not the same. Half asleep I reach and lift the phone.

"Mountain rescue callout!" I'm already up!
But mind is still cocooned in slumber's eider down.Clothes put on with practised ease.
The kettle in the kitchen sings with confidence increased. An unseen hand is filling flasks and spreading bread. She's done this vital task countless times before. It's a winter's Sunday night at ten to twelve.
Through windblown drifts our 4 x 4 ploughs up the wintry glen. A slewing, wallowing ship in a sea of driven snow. Poor souls whoever they are, that's lost in this! In the back, some would try a lurching sleep. Others tell a joke to cramped sardines. Through curried muggy air we hear their tales and share their stale and beery breath.

A lonely car waits. Like a forlorn and faithful dog in the empty yard. The creeping drifts engulf and tell that none's been near. In the black of darkest night we take to the hill. The piercing arctic gale sneers at struggling men. Its icy talons scraping clothes and face. The rhythmic beating drone of a chopper is heard above. At least we're not alone.
Through swirling drift a ghostly form appears.

Wet, cold and bewildered he cannot speak.
He tries to cry but tears they will not come.
"Where's the lassie?" anxious voices now
demand. "Out there," he gasps and whimpering, waves a frozen
hand. The tears they come at last and burn his icy cheeks. Then
sobbing heaves his frightened breast.

Above the howling wind the radio bursts forth.
"Casualty found!" Her lifeless form asleep in drifting snow. No
pulse nor breath.
At peace amidst the gale. Her open sightless eyes black pools in
an ice cold ivory face.
Among the Scottish mountain men an alien cockney voice, "Shit
or bust," the chopper's medic cries and stabs the needle in.

Engines roar. Up and away she goes through swirling wind and
snowy downdraught. Is there still a spark of life, or is her soul
already high above the storm? Soon others will take over
whilst silent brooding men make for home
down the twisted wintry glen.

With eyes tight clenched, a hot and stinging shower brings ease
to aching muscles tired and cold. The hoover stops. I hear the
ringing phone. "Aye, I'll tell him." Through the door a welcome
voice confides, "That lassie's back from the brink. She'll be
okay." The hoover starts again and busy life resumes anew.

A WINTER TRAGEDY

Jock's Road is a popular hill walking route stretching the 15 or so miles from Glen Doll at the head of Glen Clova in Angus over to Braemar in Aberdeenshire. The term "road" is a complete misnomer for the road is not a road at all and is little more than a track defined only by the constant use of hillwalkers. On the higher ground there are large stretches where the track completely disappears and to help the walker there is a series of small intermittent cairns to indicate the route. Even the slightest covering of snow will obliterate the path and those who venture onto this route in winter or thick mist must keep their wits about them otherwise they will become hopelessly lost.

The Glen Doll Estate was owned by Duncan Macpherson, a Scot who had made good in Australia and on his return to Scotland bought the estate in the latter part of the 19th. century. The route had been used for many years by those travelling between Glen Clova and Braemar and vice versa. However, Macpherson objected to travellers crossing his land and on purchasing Glen Doll, put a ban on people using the route. This ban had serious implications not only for bona fide travellers but also for the shepherds from the Braemar area who would take any sheep not sold at the Braemar spring and autumn sales over the hill to Cullow market in Glen Clova where the sheep sales were held two days after the Braemar sales. The land owner was challenged over the ban and there was a series of court cases involving the landowner and the Scottish Rights of Way Society which went all the way to the House of Lords with MacPherson eventually losing the case. This was a landmark decision and protected the rights of those who wished to walk across paths on private land that had been used for generations to link two public places. The path between Glen Doll and Braemar became known as Jock's Road after Jock Winter and the Winter Corrie in Glen Clova, popular with climbers is also named after him. Jock Winter was a shepherd on the Invercauld Estate near Braemar and regularly used the route to take sheep from Braemar to the Cullow market near Dykehead in Glen Clova.

About mid morning on Thursday, 1st., January, 1959, a group of 5 men from the Universal Hiking Club in Glasgow set off to cross Jock's Road from Braemar to meet up with family and friends at Glen Doll Youth Hostel. The group comprising James Boyle, an apprentice marine fitter from Dennistoun, Frank Daly, an executive officer with the National Assistance Board, Joseph Devlin, a plasterer from Clydebank, Harry Duffin an engineer with Rolls Royce in East Kilbride and Robert McFaul, a teacher at Coatbridge Technical College, were in good spirits as they left Braemar having spent the previous few days hillwalking in the Braemar area. They were looking forward to tackling Jock's Road and meeting up with their friends at the youth hostel in Glen Doll. The route was familiar to them as some in the group had been on the same walk some months previously.

The walk would take them about seven or eight hours depending on the weather conditions and they would be aware that the last part of the walk coming downhill into Glen Doll would be in failing light as at that time of year the sun sets around 3.45p.m. with darkness quickly following.

The last sighting of the group was by a local shepherd, Charlie Smith just after noon. At that time they were not far from his house at Auchallater and were making their way up Glen Callater towards the loch. Their route at this point was a good well defined track rising gently towards Loch Callater. They would not encounter any seriously steep ground for about 6 miles until they climbed the bealach between Creag Leachdach and Tolmount. Their route would then take them upwards to Crow Craigies which at 920 meters was the highest point of the walk. The higher ground had been covered with snow for some time and on reaching this level the walkers encountered driving snow and storm force 11 gales giving a wind chill factor of around -25C. With hindsight it would be easy to suggest that they should have made the decision to turn back. But they were already over halfway towards Glen Doll Youth Hostel where their friends were awaiting them and one can understand why they chose to carry on. Providing you are well equipped, walking through heavy snow in blizzard conditions can actually be quite warm and provided you do not become exhausted there should not be a problem. However, on that day, the group were met with the worst conditions for years in a storm that was to last for two days.

No doubt once on the tops the conditions deteriorated greatly and it would seem that after delving through deep snow the men understandably became exhausted and got overwhelmed. Given the arctic conditions, hypothermia would quickly set in but sadly not before the men came to realise that they were unlikely to survive. They would have done their utmost to carry on but one by one they eventually succumbed to the atrocious weather.

Meanwhile, their anxious friends were waiting for them at Glen Doll Youth Hostel. The road out of Glen Doll was blocked with snow and the only telephone line was down. It was Saturday, 3rd. January, before police in Forfar were made aware of the possible tragedy. A group of local gamekeepers, farmers and shepherds then carried out a fruitless search and then were joined on the Sunday by members of mountaineering clubs and mountain rescue teams in a major search co-ordinated by the police. That day, they found the body of James Boyle above the head of Glen Doll a little way off Jock's Road near Craig Maud. Thereafter the searchers continued for a further two days without finding any trace of the remaining four walkers. It was clear by that time that there was no hope of finding anyone alive and the search was called off not least because of the dangerous weather conditions.

A keen Angus Hillwalker, Davie Glen continued to search on and off when weather permitted and on Sunday, March 1st, he and some others found the body of Harry Duffin at the bottom of the White Water waterfall a short distance from where James Boyle had been found. As the weather slowly improved a greater search of the area was organised with about 80 volunteers taking part and on Saturday, March 7th. they discovered the body of Robert McFaul. He too was found near the White Water burn. Davie Glen continued his quest with some others and on Sunday, March 15th. the body of Joseph Devlin was recovered in the burn near Jock's Road about 400 yards from where Robert McFaul was discovered. However it was not until Sunday, 19th. April, that the body of Frank Daly was eventually found in a metre of snow at the upper reaches of the White Water.

After this tragedy Davie Glen was instrumental in building a shelter in the shadow of Cairn Lunkard which is known as "Davie's Bourach." It is still there to this day and is maintained by Forfar and District Hillwalking Club. A metal plaque in remembrance of the five lost hillwalkers is fixed on a rock nearby.

In the years that followed, more and more people took up the sport of climbing and hillwalking and in 1971, under the leadership of Bill Yule and Tom Deas, Angus Constabulary formed a police mountain rescue team. Tom had been one of the original police searchers in 1959. Over the years, this team took part in many searches and whilst they dealt with an increasing number of accidents and fatalities, none was on the scale of the 1959 Jock's Road tragedy.

THE MINISTER'S TWO STEP

The Reverend Malcolm Rooney is a long established and well respected Minister of The Glens and Kirriemuir Old Parish Church. At the beginning of January, 2009, he attended a party in Kirriemuir Town Hall to celebrate the 90th. Birthday of one of Kirriemuir's residents, Mrs. Annie Milne. Annie is a well known and popular lady having been involved in fund raising for the R.N.L.I. for over 50 years as well as many other local organisations. At the party, whilst taking part in a lively "Dashing White Sergeant" dance, Malcolm's Achilles tendon gave way and so gave rise to "The Ball o' Kirriemuir Mark Two" hereunder.

Whaur Catlaw's braes wi pride look doon
Upon oor wee red sandstane toon
A birthday bash wis held ye see
Twas on a Setterday, January, three.

The Toon Hall it wis packet oot
Wi auld an' young an' slim an' stoot
For Annie's birthday a' had came
Tae pey repects tae Kirrie's "Dame".

Noo Reverend Malcolm he wis there
In a meenit o' madness made a dare
"At ilky dance I'll tak the flair
My bum'll never see a chair."

He reeled an' set syne crossed an' cleekit
Wi' soaken sark o' swite he reeket
But ne'er a dance did he miss oot
Baith sound o' leg an' fleet o' foot

97

He loupet roun' in fancy style
Jist like John Sargeant for a while
Bruce Forsyth he wad be plaised
Wi' the fancy steps that Malcy yaised

But his gallusses they wernae new
The threid gaed ping a button flew
An' whilst he tried tae stop an' sit
The danglin' 'lastic reached his fit

The breeks they then began tae slide
His modesty he tried tae hide
An' grabbin' hard at front an back
He heard his tendon gie a crack

The puir auld sinew did its best
But Malcolm widnae hae a rest
Noo he's laid up an' swaithed in stookie
An' Linda's left tae preach the "Bookie"

Noo wha' this tale o' lees shall read
Ilk man an' mither's son tak' heed
That when tae dance ye are inclined
An' strathspeys or reels ging through yer mind
Jist mind the tale that I have tell't
An' as weel as gallusses, wear a belt!

THE AAL' MANNIES' SEAT

Sittin' in the recess
At the tap o' Castle Street,
There wis a lang mahogany bench
Far mannies they did meet.
Ilky day at half past ten,
Ye'd see them sittin there,
Pitten' a' the world tae richts.
In rainy days or fair.

Fa' wis mairriet, fa' wis deid
An' fa' had teen a lass.
Ilky body wis teen throwe,
Nae metter fit their class.
Each passer-by wis looket at
An' each wis scrutinised,
If they kent fa' the femily wis
They a' were criticised.

Young quines wi' their modern clyes
Cam' in for much attention.
Their lingth o' skirts and coloured hair
Got mony a cheeky mention.
An' as for bare skinned waists on view,
Each mannie rubbed his een.
They couldna' see the p'int ava'
Nor the hicht o' platform sheen.

An' files the mannies a' fell oot,
Ye'd hear them shout an sweir.
'Twis maistly aboot the politics
That een o' them held dear.
Bit afore things a' got oot o' han',
Their pals wid calm them doon.
An' spik aboot the wither,
Or far's yer aal'est loon?

Fin peace at last hid broken oot
They a' sat quate a file.
Syne spoke aboot the young folk noo
Or ' fa wis in the jile.
At twal' o'clock they a' steed up,
Then each een made for hame.
An' if his tattie soup wis caal'
The ithers got the blame.

POPPIES

Dotted red in fields of corn
Scarlet poppies sway forlorn.
Petals for women and the men,
Their lives cut short from hill and glen.

From village small and busy city
All turned out to do their duty.
Names well known and ne'er forgot,
Some distant field is now their lot.

Yet still each year more poppies grow
With new names added row on row.
If only we could use our power
To make each poppy just a flower.

GRUNNY'S CLOCKS

Grunny's hoose wis fu' o' clocks
They were on ilky wa'.
Some were on the mantelpiece
An' chests o' draa'rs an' a'.

Ilky een said tick- a- tock
An' some lat oot lang chimes.
Tho' affen were they a' w'un' up,
Each een telt diff'rent times.

Her fav'rite een wis timmer made,
It hid nae funcy gless.
It hung abeen the mantelpiece
Richt next tae Granda's press.

It hid a cuckoo bidin' there,
He sprung oot ahin' a door,
An' shouted oot the time o' day
As he'd affen deen afore.

Grunny had it a' her days
Since she had left the skweel.
She said it cam' fae Aikey Fair
Fin she wis young an' feel.

Her clocks they hiv a' stoppit noo
Bit een still ticks awa',
An' that's her ain aal' cuckoo clock
That's hingin' on ma wa'.

NO WAY TO TREAT A LADY

In the 1950's many farmers in Aberdeenshire relied on itinerant workers to help with the grain harvest, potato planting and gathering and also thinning the turnip crop. Nowadays such workers would be referred to as "Travelling People" but in those days they were all simply called "Tinks." Whilst this term may have caused offence to those to whom it was directed, it was not meant to be derogatory but was simply the way that most people spoke at that time.

There were great families or clans of travellers, Stewarts, McPhees, Williamsons, Townsleys, Whytes and so on. They were a recognised ethnic group some being the remnants of dispossessed families following the 1745 Jacobite Rebellion. Many of them still spoke Gaelic and many of the women folk would wear tartan shawls. Because many of them shared the same surname and forename, nicknames were common much like the fisher communities of the north-east. For example, nicknames such as "Reid Wullie" or "Fite Jimmy" arose from the hair colour of men sharing the same forename and family surname.

One such man, Hector Johnstone, was nicknamed "Hecky Bloo E'e" So called because he had a blue glass eye. His good eye was brown and the story went that Hector had been in the Gordons during the war and had lost an eye after being wounded at El Alamein. He had been fitted with a blue glass eye perhaps because there had been a shortage of brown glass eyes during the war. Whatever the reason, the nickname Hecky Bloo E'e stuck to him. Hecky was married to Harriet (Hattie) Stewart. She was a formidable woman from a long line of tinkers from the Aberdeen area . She was not pretty and had lived an eventful life which was reflected in her ruddy weather beaten face and the few stumps of tobacco stained teeth that still graced her terracotta gums. Whether Hecky and Hattie were actually married we do not know but they called themselves man and wife and may well have gone through some sort of campfire ceremony according to their culture.

Anyway, in the early summer of 1955, Hecky and Hattie were engaged in piece work hyowin' neeps on a farm near St Fergus. It was a very hot day and by late afternoon the pair were tired, dusty and thirsty and after collecting their wages, purchased six "screw tops" of pale ale and a half bottle of whisky from a travelling licensed grocer's van. They then would walk back towards Rora Moss where their camp was, sampling their purchase as they travelled. Not having eaten for some time, the alcohol quickly took effect. To a casual observer seeing their jovial happy mood it was quite apparent that the pair had had a "refreshment". Their mood slowly changed however when they reminisced over some sad events in their lives, embraced each other and became quite emotional. "Greetin' fu' ". some would say. By the time they reached the small hamlet of Bridgend, known locally as Briggies, the pair of them were completely "oot o' the shewin", had fallen out and were arguing in a rather loud and aggressive fashion - a not uncommon feature of their tempestuous relationship. By this time they were halfway across the high narrow Bridgend Bridge which spans the River Ugie some 30 feet below. The pair continued to shout, swear and gesticulate at each other much to the alarm and annoyance of the good people of Briggies who promptly phoned the Police. The arguing and shouting continued then suddenly and without warning Hattie lifted up her skirts, divested herself of her knickers and with a defiant flourish dropped the garment over the parapet of the bridge whereby it wafted gently down to the waters below. Hecky stared at this in stunned disbelief, then completely lost the plot punching Hattie full in the face. At this point the Constabulary arrived in the form of two brosie Buchan bobbies who enquired, "Aye, Aye, fit's gaan on here?" They then promptly arrested Hecky for breach of the peace and assault and Hattie for breach of the peace. Both were carted off to languish in the cells at Peterhead until court the next day.

Now, no one ever found out why Hattie had behaved in such a strange and peculiar fashion or why her actions had provoked such violent behaviour from her husband. Perhaps her actions had some deep seated meaning in Tinker culture. Perhaps whoever recovered the garment could claim some favour from the owner. Who knows?

The next day and by now somewhat subdued, the pair were put in the back of a police van to be taken to court. By this time, as was often the case, the couple had made up and all was forgiven. Terms of endearment were being exchanged and with all the tenderness he could muster, Hecky was telling Hattie what he intended to do to her "Eence I get ye back tae the tent."! Hattie gave a coy toothy smile and bowed her head in feigned embarrassment whilst the two escorting police officers shuddered at the prospect of what they imagined was later to ensue.

The court was in respectful silence as the two appeared in the dock and pled guilty. Alexander S. Ingles, the respected and long standing Procurator Fiscal rose to his feet and outlined the facts of the case to resident Sheriff, Harold Frank Hillman. Sheriff Hillman had sat on the bench at Peterhead for many years and this was by no means the first time that Hecky and Hattie had appeared before his Lordship. He fined Hattie £5 for breach of the peace - a fairly substantial sum in 1955. The Sheriff then turned his attention to Hecky. "Johnstone," he said in his cultured Oxford voice, "I take a very dim view of any man who would strike a lady and particularly so when that lady happens to be your wife." "What have you got to say for yourself?"

Now the Sheriff was perhaps being a little generous in describing Hattie as a "lady". Bear in mind, she had been drunk the day before and had a serious hangover. Her hair was tousled, she had bloodshot eyes and was sporting a black eye. She had been working in a dusty neep field and her clothes were crumpled and covered in stue. She had no knickers on. Nevertheless I suppose

104

the Sheriff was technically correct describing her as a "lady."

Hecky Bloo E'e rose to his feet in the dock. He had done this countless times before. Being an old soldier, he pulled himself up to his full height, chin in, chest out, fists clenched with the thumbs pointing down the seams of his trousers. He stared straight ahead and addressed the Sheriff. The court could see that he was reliving the moment of his downfall and the anger again rose within him. Through gritted teeth he uttered, "Weell ma Lord, it's jist like 'iss, fit kine o' a wuman taks aff 'er briks an' throws 'em ower Briggies brig?" "If your wife hid deen 'at, wid you nae hae punched her face?" The public benches erupted in stifled laughter. The Sheriff kept a straight if somewhat reddened face but did not enlighten the court as to what he would have done if the genteel and fragrant Penelope Hillman should ever have done such a thing Instead, his shoulders could be seen to rise and fall in quick succession causing his wig to go slightly askew.

Regaining his composure, the Sheriff cleared his throat and addressed Hecky. "I fine you £15 Johnstone." "That was no way to treat a lady!"

BESSIE'S WAALL

Bessie's Waall, named after Bessie Davidson, also known as Dav'son's Waall (well), is not a well at all but a natural spring of clear, cold, fresh water not far from Blackhills on the outskirts of Peterhead.

Ben the road fae Craigie's craft
A larch stan's stracht an taall.
There is a spring o' waatter near
That's kent as Bessie's Waall.

In bygane times there stood a hoose
Its gairden eence kept neat
But a' that's left are mossy steens
An' honeysuckle sweet.

Weary hackers aft wid stop
Tae tak the watter caal.
A sweeter sup they ne'er could get
Than een fae Bessie's Waall.

Bairnies comin fae the skweel
Wid stop an' drink their fill.
Syne step the road for hame again
At the tap o' Rodgers hill.

An aftimes noo as I think back
As ye div fin you are aal',
I min' o' freen's lang syne gane
That drank fae Bessie's Waall.

GLOBAL WARMING

Having been brought up on a farm I have a great affinity with nature and the countryside.   Much is now being said about climate change and global warming.   There are those who tell us that it is all our fault due to our modern lifestyle of air travel, use of motor vehicles etc.   No doubt these are honest views sincerely held and should be respected. I'm pretty relaxed about the whole thing and think that it is mostly down to nature.   In the past, the earth has gone through successive periods of natural global warming and cooling - the ice ages.   What we are experiencing now may be just part of the ongoing pattern of climate change, the cycles of which could be many hundreds or even thousands of years long.   That said, we should all look after the scarce resources of our planet as best we can for future generations.

My bleed is thin an' I'm gettin' aal'
My taes an' fing'ers aye feel 'i caal'
Bit I shouldna' worry 'cos it disnae metter
For a'body says the world is hetter.

The Polar ice has begun ti' milt
Bit it's still ower caal' tae weer ma' kilt
I like 'i heater oan in cars
Bit I wunna' tak' aff ma' winter draars.

It's April month an' 'i sna's still here
An' it's efterneen or 'i frost is clear
The pavement slush it qweels ma' feet
So I've yet ti' fin' some sign o' heat.

Bit is it me or them that's wrang
Is oor wither aff 'i fang?
Tho' ithers say it's het an' bleezin'
I'm stunnin' here an' bluiddy freezin'.

AUTUMN

Golden fields of stooks in rows,
On highest hills a dust of snows.
Apples red on bended bough,
September days pass quickly now.

Cooler air with skies deep blue,
A skein of geese comes into view.
And floating in the zephyred breeze
The seeds of summer glide with ease.

Sparkling webs in morning dew
Give woodland walks a tinselled hue.
And trees that once were clad in green
Add red and yellow to the scene.

Soaring high in highland air
An eagle hunts with deadly stare.
The crags resound with rutting deer
As creeping mists tell autumn's here.

TIN LIZZIE

Lizzie wis a sheet o' iron,
corrugated aff a reef.
Blaa'n doon in squally wither,
Tossed aboot like autumn leaf.

A' forgotten, lyin' roostin'
Fu' o' holes an' nae mair ease.
Trailled awa' by three young laddies
The treasures in their den increase.

Left aleen till days o' winter,
Sna' on braes is lyin' deep.
Laddies syne they wakin' Lizzie
Fae her lang forgotten sleep.

Up the frozen hill they drag 'er.
Boo her front jist like a sleigh.
Tak' a rin an' jump in ower 'er,
Syne gang hurtlin' doon the brae.

Dirdin' fast ower snavvie hillocks.
Crashin' throwe the deepest drift,
Yells an' lachter fae the laddies.
Nivver thocht she'd be sae swift.

A' ower quick they reach the boddem
Roll aboot richt oot o' breath.
Imagine they are spitfire pilots
Back to base and cheated death.

THE DRYSTEEN DYKE

Draystane dykes or dry stone walls are a common feature of Scotland particularly so in the northern and upland areas where the weather is harsh and too severe for hedges or trees to grow. They are so called "dry stane" because no cement or mortar was used in their construction. Such methods were used for thousands of years as protection against intruders or wild animals. Latterly they were used to confine livestock in fields or to mark the march boundary of neighbouring estates. Many of the drystane dykes standing today date from the 18th. century or later.

The hands that built ye lang since geen
Wi cannae care they placed each steen.
Twa hunner years ye've stood in line
A monument o' times lang syne.

Through winters lang an' dreich an' caald
Yer steens have stood whilst we growe aald.
We little thocht o' you oot there
When we were young withoot a care.

But noo we're age'd bent an grey
Oor simmer's past it's langest day
But lang an' stracht your wa's still stan'
Superior now to mortal man.

WINTER

Silent flakes fall through the night
Make altered scenes in morning light,
As open curtains start to show
That all around is white with snow.

A heavy sky of leaden grey
Assures that more is on the way.
Now songbirds beg at garden tables
As greedy jackdaws watch from gables.

Short cold days with longer dark
Naked trees stand in the park.
Their leafless twigs reach to the sky
As flying geese give mournful cry

Snow clad sheep in hilly field
Seek shelter in a dry stone bield.
A frosty sky begins to clear
And twinkling stars tell winter's here.

MITHER TONGUE

Although I only spent the first four years of my life in Buchan I tend
to speak with a Buchan accent when in the company of my "ain folk".
My Kirriemuir grandchildren think this is very strange and have a
giggle when I call them "quines" and tell them to "Tie their pints."

"Where were you born Grandad?"
My little quine did speir
"Weel, I wis born in Ellon.
It's nae that far fae here."

"But is it still in Scotland?"
She asked in a puzzled way.
"It's in the hert o' Buchan lass,
I'm affa' prood tae say."

"Bit foo are ye speirin' that ma dear,
It's hard for me tae see?"
"Well you sound kind of foreign,
For you don't speak like me".

An' so she made me think a bit
An' she's richt in fit she says,
For bairnies a' spik "proper" noo.
Nae like in my young days.

I hear them comin' fae the skweel
An' I listen as they walk.
Neen o' them spiks broad ava',
It's jist a' "proper" talk.

Noo whether 'at is gweed or bad
It's nae for me tae say.
But mony aal' Scots words are lost
Tae the bairnies of today.

Noo fin I like, I can spik richt.
But I hope you will agree,
I much prefer the aal Scots tongue
I learnt on mither's knee.

THE RURAL

The Scottish Women's Rural Institute was founded in 1917. Among other things, its aims are the advance and education of those who live or work in the country by encouraging home skills and preserving the traditions of rural Scotland. Today, there are S.W.R.I. institutes in most small towns, villages and country communities.

Eence a month on Thursday nicht
She's in a steer tae get things richt.
So I lie low till I hear the cry,
"That's me awa' tae the W.R.I."

Competitions then they wull tak' place.
Ye'd think it wis a vital race.
A jar o' jam or slice o' cake,
That forty wifies hiv tae bake.

The judge will be an ootside guest,
An' has tae pick which een is best.
Lord help 'im if he gets it wrang,
For ower the couples he micht hang!

For Rural wifies it's serious stuff,
'An' some o' them ging in the huff
If their mango chutney or wild game pie
Has failed tae tak' the umpire's eye.

An' me at hame ma leen, fit rare.
A while at the telly I wull stare,
Or read the paper an' fa' asleep.
I hiv nae need for coontin' sheep.

Bit a' ower soon I hear the door.
Wis I supposed tae dae some chore?
"That's me back." I hear her cry
"I won first prize at the W.R.I."

SNARES

Growing up on a farm in the 1950's was an idyllic way to spend a childhood. There was always something to take up the interests of a growing laddie. With my pal Ian from next door, we would go for long walks through the fields and woods, guddle for trout in the burns and explore the nearby hills. There was a single man called Henry who stayed in the farm bothy and he taught us how to catch rabbits. Once we went with Henry to look for pheasants eggs. I would have been about 8 and Ian would have been about 12. We trespassed onto a neighbouring farm and duly found and took some eggs. The next thing we knew, we were confronted by the angry farmer. "Aye, and what are you lads up to?" he enquired. Being the youngest, I kept my mouth firmly shut and looked to my elders for salvation. Before Henry had a chance to offer an excuse Ian proudly proclaimed, "We're oot lookin' for pheasants eggs." "Have you found any?" asked the farmer. "Aye." said Ian. "And where are they?" enquired the farmer. "They're in aneth Henry's bonnet." said Ian more truthfully than wisely. A quick glance at Henry's bonnet revealed a number of rounded tell-tale bumps that gave credence to Ian's confession! "Well you'd better just go and put them back." said the farmer. Now, I can't remember if Henry kicked a certain part of Ian's anatomy on the way home or not but never again did we go out looking for pheasants' eggs with Henry. Here is a poem as a reminder of those happy times which passed all too soon.

Did ivver ye rise
wi' the day's new licht,
As a bricht mornin' sun
says fareweel tae the nicht.

Syne stridet throwe parks
A' glistenin' wi' dew,
Saw the wonders o' nature
On a day that wis new.

114

Jist a loon an' his dog
Awa' tae their snares,
Ower aal' tae play games,
Ower young tae hae cares.

Tae watch a roe deer
In the mist covered howe,
Oh! affen I wish
I could still dee that now.

A fox he rins bye,
He's been in amon' hens.
Far he's cam' fae
There's naebody kens.

Bit some fermer's wife
Wull wakin richt seen
An' ken that her hennies
A foxy has teen.

Syne doon tae the wuid
Wi' its ha'thorn hedge,
An' twa dizzen snares
Set a' roon' the edge.

Wi' a rubbit or twa
An' a fine big broon hare,
Eneuch for twa suppers,
Ye couldna ask mair.

Then hame tae the hoose
An' a quick bowl o' brose,
A dicht wi the face cloot
An' on wi' school clothes.

Syne aff doon the road
Wi' a glint in yer e'e,
For the nicht there's roast rubbit
An' skirlie for tea!

CAIN AND ABEL

It is many years since corporal punishment was abolished in Scottish schools. There was a time however when most teachers possessed and administered punishment with a leather belt or strap. In Buchan, the belt was called "the tag." These belts were custom made of brown or black leather about 2 feet long with two or sometimes three tails. They were manufactured by a firm in Lochgelly, Fife, and known as the Lochgelly Tawse. In times gone by, when properly used by responsible teachers, the tawse was a quick and effective way of maintaining discipline in class by way of a short sharp lesson. Most children, having been given the belt, quickly learned the error of their ways and did not require a second dose. That said, there were a few teachers who went over the score. I can remember being in Primary 7 and witnessing a classmate being given 22 strokes of the belt all on the one hand! His crime - he had collected a number of live beetles and during the lesson he dropped them onto the head of the girl in front of him who got a fright and went into hysterics. He certainly deserved to be punished but not thrashed to that extent. Perhaps it is just as well that the tawse has disappeared from our schools.

Oor dominie wis a fearsome chiel
He ruled wi' an iron rod
An' in oor little country skweel
There's nae doot he wis God.

The quines they were a' feart at him,
He affen made them greet.
A sharp word or an angry glower
It scared each cowrin' geet.

The loons made on they didna' care
Bit ilky een wis shakkin'
If the mannie tell't them tae come oot
Fae the tag tae get their whakkin'.

He had twa he affen used
An' ca'ed them Cain and Abel.
Each een wis ledder, black as nicht.
Aal' harness fae some stable.

An' oh! they garr't yer fing'ers dirl
If you hid geen some chik.
Wi' lang reid marks on baith yer han's
that hurted for a wik.

Bit country loons growe big an' strong
Fin fed wi' brose an' meal,
An' there comes a time fin they look doon
On the dominie at their skweel.

They mine' the times he leddert them
An' left their fing'ers sair.
Syne contermashious youth sets in
An' then they'll tak' nae mair.

So on the hin'maist day o' term
They teen revenge sae sweet
For Cain an' Abel they cut up
An' gart the dominie greet.

DINNA BE COORSE TAE LITTLE LOONS
(From an old Buchan saying)

"Dinna be coorse tae little loons,
For little loons growe up an' kick mens' airses".

SLAINS CASTLE

The ruins of Slains Castle stand on the rocky Buchan coast just off the B1345 road near Cruden Bay and is some 24 miles north east of Aberdeen. The castle ruins are a prominent feature of the coastal landscape and can be seen from many miles around. The original building was built in 1597 by Francis Hay, 9th. Earl of Errol. It was altered and extended over the years and substantially rebuilt and faced with granite in 1836 forming a modern country house. It was sold in 1916 by the 20th. Earl to help pay death duties, then 9 years later the roof was removed having become unsafe. It is said that Bram Stoker, author of Dracula gained the inspiration for his novel when he visited the castle in 1895. Today the castle ruins still look impressive clinging to the edge of sheer rocky cliffs and are a focal point for tourists and walkers. Until I was 4 years old we lived at Slains Lodge farm which is just a field away from the castle and I remember being taken for walks there on Sunday afternoons.

Fa bigget ye, wi' hard granite steen?
Twal' generations yer sturdy wa's hae seen.
Stannin' prood on Cruden's coast,
A shelter for a hameless ghost.
On tap o' rugged heughs o' green
the sea below, the sky abeen.

Yer gables mock each ragin' gale
An' dar' each storm tae you assail.
Through empty windaes drives the blast
Wi' frothy seas yer steens are splashed.
But still ye stan', a stagin' post
on Buchan's rocky win' swept coast.

Far, far back in mists o' time,
Coontless feet yer stairs did climb.

Slains Castle, Cruden Bay, Aberdeenshire.
Picture by Allan J.R. Thomson

Wi' Lairds an' Ladies they did share
Banquets fu' o' gweed Scotch fare.
But them that dwelt an' them that came
Hae lang since reached a higher hame.

Yet still the wa's o' granite wait.
For maybe there are some that's late.
But a' that come jist stan' an' stare
An' wonder who an' what was there.
An' fa kens fit the walker thinks
As he stan's an' stares at Cruden's Sphinx.

RAINY TUESDAY

It's rainy Tuesday, michty me,
An' I hiv sic a lot tae dee.
I ken fit'll happen if I ging oot,
A soakin' fae yon broken spoot.
Ma briks'll a' get splashed wi cars
An' I'll end up wi' wringin' draars.

Noo I should rise an' tax ma car
Or I'll get nabbed which will be waur.
Bit I'm affa swiert tae leave ma seat,
An' ging ootside an' end up weet.
The watters rise fae ilky drain,
It's jist a day o' pishin' rain.

Wi han's in pooches I walk the fleer
An' the posties late again I fear.
The paper loon has missed oor street
An' ony mair wull gar ma greet.
I kick ma heels and I'm foot loose.
Ach, I think I'll bide 'ee hoose.

GREEN DEUK AIGGS

It was well kent in the little village of Seggieden just outside the Broch that Jocky Warrender wis a bit o' a rogue. "He'd swick his ain grunny oot o' a shillin," said some. Others being somewhat kinder, described Jocky as a rough diamond, "That nivver did naebody ony hairm." No one knew exactly where Jocky had come from. In the early fifties he was over retirement age and lived in a little croft known locally as The Herrin Craft but how it came by that name nobody was quite sure. It was Jocky's wife Nellie, that actually owned the croft as it had belonged to her parents and grandparents.

Jocky was a small wiry individual and unfortunately for him, had the shifty look of a small time crook. If he had been asked to take part in an identification parade the chances were that he would have been picked out whether innocent or not. He had done a number of dead end jobs but towards the end of the war had got employment as a civilian handyman at Crimond Airfield which had just opened. Jocky remained there until he retired in 1946 which coincided with the airfield ceasing its military role. It was during his time there that Jocky got the reputation of being a rascal. If anyone in the village wanted anything that was difficult to come by they would go to Jocky who usually managed to acquire it for them. It was said at that time that "Half the men in Seggie were weerin' R.A.F. sarks and every barn door for miles aroon wis pented R.A.F. blue.

Although now retired, Jocky was aye on the lookout to make a bob or two. He was no crofter though and left that sort of thing to Nellie. They had a field, byre and outhouse and kept a cow, hens and ducks selling butter, eggs and home made cheese. One day whilst in the local butchers shop, Jocky noticed that when buying duck eggs, folk would speir at the butcher. "Hiv ye ony green eens Bill, I aye think they taste better". Bill Mackie had ran the butchers shop in Seggieden since taking over from his father at the end of the war. Bill confided to Jocky, "There's nae difference in the taste ye ken, they're a' the same fite or green. Maybe I should chairge an extra fowerpence a dizzen for the green eens." Thus was planted a seed in Jocky's mind.

A week later, a sign appeared nailed to a strainer post at the end of the Herrin Craft road, "Green Duck Eggs For Sale." In no time at all Nellie noticed an increase in the numbers of her customers and of course Jocky had told her, "Ye'd better chairge an extra fowerpence or so a dizzen for the green eens," which she duly did. This went well for a short while but all too soon Nellie had run out of green eggs and had to turn customers away. Seeing people leaving the croft empty handed save for some butter and a hame made cheese or the cheaper white duck eggs was just too much for Jocky to bear so he set about remedying the situation. After a while Nellie remarked to him that, "The deuks are layin' affa weel, I've nivver kent them tae lay sae much." The other mystery was that now all the eggs were green whereas in the past, out of her twelve ducks there were only three that she knew of that laid green eggs. Such too was the surplus of eggs that Jocky was even supplying them to Bill Mackie the butcher. It was a situation that Nellie could not fathom out but Jocky had never been happier so she kept her own counsel. However, rumours were rife that Jocky had been seen scourin the Broch and ilky craft in atween there an Seggie for deuk aiggs.

Now it so happened that a new bobby who had just joined the force had been posted to the Broch. Bill Catto had come from Inverurie and had no knowledge of the Broch or its surrounding area. One evening in October just as the nights were drawing in, his sergeant, George Burnett said to him, "C'mon Bill, we'll tak a look oot by Seggie an see fits gaan on ere." Geordie Burnett was an old school bobby who had joined the force several years before the war and then went off to fight with the Gordon Highlanders. On demob in 1946 he re-joined and after a spell at Peterhead, was promoted and went to the Broch as a sergeant where he had been for the last five years.   He was a big strong built man with a moustache and displayed an impressive array of medal ribbons on his tunic from his wartime service.   It was well known throughout the area that Sergeant Burnett's authoritative appearance was all that was required to have an immediate and soothing effect on any local youths who were on the verge of causing trouble whether at a village dance or out on the street.

Sergeant Burnett knew of Jocky Warrender although their paths had never crossed in a professional capacity but good canny bobby that he was, he had heard whispers about the green deuk aiggs at Seggie.   When the two bobbies arrived in the village they had a walk round and George pointed out the various places of interest to the new probationer.   Being just after 9 p.m., it was quite dark and as they turned the corner into the village square they noticed that four or five people were gathered outside the butchers looking intently in at the window.   "Aye, aye lads, fit like the nicht." said the sergeant.   "A' weel we're juist gie curious," remarked Tom Kelman the postie.   "Oh, an fit mith ye be curious aboot Toam?" queried the sergeant.   "Green deuk aiggs," replied the postie.   "Aye we are 'at," murmered the other onlookers.   "Juist tak a look at that bowl o' them on the butcher's shelf George, the bluiddy things are a' lichtet up."   Sergeant Burnett peered into the darkened shop and sure enough sitting on a shelf was a bowl filled with duck eggs but stranger still was the fact that the eggs seemed to be emitting a low greenish light.   "I'll better juist ging an hae a word wi Bill Mackie, the butcher," said the sergeant.   "I'm gie sure there'll be a simple explanation.   Noo than, you lads should juist hud on hame up the road."

Bill Mackie lived above the shop and Sergeant Burnett waited a minute or two until the postie and his companions were away before knocking on the butcher's door.   "Oh it's yersel George," said the butcher as he opened the door.   "Fit can I dee for ye the nicht?"   "Ye can come an hae a look in throwe yer windae," said the sergeant.   He indicated the bowl of glowing eggs and said,

"Noo than Bill, fit div ye mak o' that?" For a moment Bill Mackie was open mouthed and speechless. He eventually replied, "Goad almichty, I dinna ken fit's gaan on ere. I bocht 'at aiggs fae Jocky Warrender. He's sell't me a dizzen or so iss last wik or twa." "We'd better tak a closer look at em," said the sergeant. The two bobbies followed the butcher into the shop and the eggs were taken upstairs to the kitchen of the house where upon closer examination, they looked to be quite normal. However on taking the bowl into the darkened lobby, a distinct glow could be seen coming from the eggs. "I hinna hid ony complints fae customers," said the puzzled butcher. "Div ye want tae try een or twa?" "Aye, we micht as weel," said the sergeant. Six eggs were put in a pot and brought to the boil. After a few minutes they were taken out and the butcher produced egg cups, butter and oatcakes and Bill Catto, Sergeant Burnett and the butcher all sat down to sample the eggs. The breid was buttered and the serious business of sampling the eggs commenced. Nothing was said for a minute or so and then the butcher spoke first. "Weel, I'm damned if I can fin' onything wrang wi them." "Me neither," said the young constable." Na, na, they're richt eneuch tasted." said the sergeant. The three of them sat in silence considering the situation for a moment or two then unseen by the young constable, the butcher gave the sergeant a knowing look. "Bill, ye mith step ootside an juist mak sure a' thing's a' richt on the street," said the sergeant. "I'll be oot in a meenty." When the young constable had gone Bill Mackie rose up and on opening the sideboard door produced a bottle of Long John whisky and two glasses which he filled with generous measures. "Here's luck," said the butcher. "Cheers" said the sergeant and both men downed their drinks. "I'll maybe better tak the half dizzen aiggs that's left as evidence." said the sergeant on leaving. "Aye, juist help yersel," said the butcher.

The next morning bright and early, Sergeant Burnett and Constable Catto arrived at the Herrin Craft. They entered the outhouse and took Jocky completely by surprise as he was transferring duck eggs from a cardboard box onto a bench. He reddened as the visitors came in. "Aye Jocky," said the sergeant. "Fit are ye up till the day?" "Naething ava," Jocky replied guiltily. "I'm juist sortin oot some o' ma deuk aiggs." " 'At's fit we're here tae see ye aboot Jocky," said the sergeant enjoying his game of cat and mouse with the clearly uncomfortable Jocky. "Oh aye." said Jocky hanging his head. "Aye," said the sergeant, "Wid ye sell each o's a dizzen?" "Oh, nae buther at a' Sergeant Burnett," said Jocky almost collapsing with relief. He started to count out two dozen eggs from the cardboard box. "Ah bit we're nae wuntin fite eens," said the sergeant. "We're sicken yer green eens. We've been tell't there's a big demand for em." "Right ye are," replied Jocky and reached for a box under the bench that contained green eggs. With shaking hands he started to count out the green eggs. "Fit else is 'at aneth yer bench Jocky?" asked the sergeant as he bent down and took out a large tin that had streaks of green paint on its side where it had run down and dried . Sergeant Burnett placed the tin on the bench and read the label out loud. "War Department 1942, Luminous Paint - Green - Property of His Majesty's Government" "Noo far wid this hae come fae Jocky?" asked the sergeant. "It cam fae Crimond aerodrome," admitted a hesitant and nervous Jocky. "An fit wid it hae been used for?" continued the sergeant. "They eassed tae pent the tips o' Spitfire's wings wi it," said Jocky." "An foo wid it hae gotten tae the Herrin Craft?" queried the sergeant. "I juist took it hame wi's fin the 'drome closed." said Jocky. "Fit for?" said the sergeant. "There'll be nae Spitifires here that needs penten." The sergeant had taken out his tobacco knife and started to scrape the paint off one of the green eggs revealing the white shell below. "I'm affa sorry Sergeant Burnett," said a trembling Jocky. "Wull I get the jile?" "Oh I dinna ken aboot 'at Jocky," said the stern faced sergeant. "Pinchin government property's gie serious. Gie near as serious as treason." "Oh me." wailed a clearly distressed Jocky. Sergeant Burnett winked at the young constable, "Noo Jocky, fit's Bill an me due ye for the aiggs." "Naething ava, no naething ava," spluttered Jocky.

The two bobbies picked up their eggs and as they were about to go out of the door Sergeant Burnett turned to Jocky and said, "Noo Jocky, ye'll nae be sellin ony mair pented aiggs." No, I wunna that sergeant," said Jocky. "An anither thing," said the sergeant. " 'At sign at the ain o' yer road that says, Green Deuk Aiggs for Sale, ye'll tak that doon inna." Aye, I wull 'at," said a compliant Jocky. "Ye see," added the sergeant, "Yer sign's wrang. Yer deuks are juist the same colour as abody else's." This last comment however went completely over the head of a relieved but very subdued Jocky.

SIC EASTER SIC 'EAR

Before the days of sophisticated weather forecasting, generations of people who relied on the land or the sea for their livelihood used many different ways to try and foretell the weather. One of the most well known is of course "Red sky at night, shepherds' delight." There were many other perhaps lesser known ways that people tried to second guess the weather. For example they would observe nature and watch crows building their nests. If they built high up in the trees the weather was supposed to be reasonably calm and fine but if nests were built lower down then that meant that stormy weather could be expected. One ditty hundreds of years old related to St. Swithin. If it rained on his feast day (15th. July) then it was supposed to rain for the next 40 days! In rural Buchan the country folk had a saying, "Sic Easter, sic 'ear." (Such Easter, such year) meaning whatever the weather at Easter then similar could be expected the whole year.

Tho' Easter comes at diff'rent times
The spring's aye late in northern climes
But early Easter or een that's late
Lats fermer chiels ken o' their fate
Coorse widder at that time they fear
For "Sic an Easter, sic an 'ear."

THE AAL PEAT STACK

Whilst food and shelter would be at the top of the priority list for many country people in Scotland, fuel for the fire would also be a priority. Without fuel, food could not be cooked and homes, however humble, could not be heated. In the days when cooking was done on the open peat fire, the fire was never out - even in the height of summer - there being no other means of cooking. At night, peat dross would be placed over the glowing embers and the fire would smoulder away until morning when it would be given a rake out, then some small pieces of peat would be placed on it and in no time the fire would be burning brightly. Many older folk cannot recall seeing their fire unlit. From their earliest recollections until adulthood, their peat fires had burned continuously day and night. Peats were cast (dug out) from the many peat mosses in early summer, laid out to dry and then carted home. When taken home either by barrow or horse and cart, the peats were built into a peat stack which was close to the house. The peat stack was about the same shape as an upturned boat, reached as high as the eaves of a cottage and was built in such a way, overlapping like roof tiles, that the rain ran down the outside. The peats below the first lair were always dry and usable.

Lang, lang ago fin I wis young
I'll tell ye it's a fac',
Ilky placie hid its coo
As weel's its ain peat stack.

A chessel stood at each back door
Fine hame made cheese tae mak',
An' roon' the neuk nae far awa'
There stood the aal' peat stack.

On picnic days fae Mormon hill
We sa' them dotted black,
At crafts an' placies roon' aboot
Wis aye a big peat stack.

But times hiv changed an' noo'adays
There's North Sea gas tae tak'.
But I aften think o' happy days
Aroon' the aal peat stack.

OOT O' THE SHEWIN

Many of our old Scottish expressions are falling into disuse and are disappearing. "Oot o' the shewin" is one such example. Nowadays it is used to describe someone who is in a state of dishevelled inebriation through drink - in other words drunk and incapable. The literal translation is "Out of the sewing" and the saying stems from a time when young girls played with rag dolls. These dolls often had porcelain faces but their bodies, arms and legs were made of cloth and stuffed with rags. The dolls would be passed from child to child down through the years and after much usage they became rather tatty. Inevitably, the sewing at the seams would break and the internal stuffing would begin to show with the doll taking on a rather dilapidated appearance. At such times an adult might say to the child, "Yer dally's a' oot o' the shewin" and so the expression was born. It later came to describe anything that was rather the worse for wear and in modern times, someone who was drunk.

Geordie Broon had an affa drooth
Fuskie or beer it a' gaed sooth.
Staggerin hame cowken an spewin,
Geordie Broon wis oot o' the shewin.

Geordie Broon he hadnae a wife
Nae sensible deem wid pit up wi the strife.
He nivver had time for coortin nor wooin
For Geordie aye wis oot o' the shewin.

Geordie Broon he's lang syne deid.
He'd raether teen drink than hae a richt feed.
Ower muckle booze wis peer Geordie's ruin.
We'll see him nae mair oot o' the shewin.

10 DOWNING STREET

In 1964 I joined the Metropolitan Police and was stationed at Cannon Row Police Station just off Whitehall. Downing Street was just a matter of yards away and I frequently did duty on the door of number 10. Duty there could be interesting during the day with the comings and goings of cabinet ministers etc. However, on night shift it could get rather boring and the duty constables would devise all sorts of ways to pass the time. As a young lad I liked to carve my initials on trees and so the door of No. 10 was a quite a challenge. In the wee small hours I scratched a tiny "A" at the bottom of the number "1" and then a tiny "T" at the bottom of the zero. The initials were too small to be noticed by anyone entering No. 10, but I had the satisfaction of knowing they were there!

Had they ivver seen the like afore?
A Buchan Bobby on the door.
Wi' briks fine pressed an polished sheen
Jist new trained an' affa' keen.

Tae guard the premier wis my task
My public face a gie stern mask.
But deep deep doon I had a fear,
Fit the hell am I deein here!

Noo through the day wis a busy chore,
There wis a' kine's gaed through the door.
Important mannies wi' lots tae say,
An' a little fat quine tae mak' their tay

Bit late at nicht things quaetened doon,
An' tae amuse masel' I looked aroon'.
I bet its nivver been deen afore,
A bobby's initials on that door!

10 Downing Street

I raked ma pooches for ma knife,
The een I'd cairriet a' ma life.
But in that toon that nivver sleeps
Ther's nae a lot o' Sweddish neeps.

So my knifie it wis left at hame
An' I'd naething left tae carve ma name.
But syne I mine't aboot ma fussle
So I jist used a bit o' muscle.

I teen it aff its silver chine
Its fine sharp edge wid dee jist fine.
My initials syne I scratched wi' glee,
First an "A" and then a "T".

But that wis forty years an' mair
An' I winn'er noo if they're still there.
On T.V. news I try an' see
But there's nae sign o' my "A" or "T"

In October, 2008, the above poem was performed by Stephen Robertson of "Scotland The What" before The Prince of Wales and The Duchess of Rothesay at a private dinner party held in Fyvie Castle.

THE ROBIN

When beady brambles black as night
Are jammed and jarred and out of sight.
As arctic geese the cold skies wedge
Shy robin sits on low branched hedge.

With summer days now long forgot
These balmy times we saw him not.
Now damp dark days chill to the core
Shy robin hops to cottage door.

Each rowan tree ablaze with red.
There's falling leaves for squirrel's bed
As homeward children trudge along
Shy robin trills a mournful song.

THE NEEP

Nowadays, youngsters get into trouble if they carry knives - and quite right too. When I was young, the world was a different place and every young country loon carried a pocket knife - it was an essential part of the contents of a wee lad's pooch. You never knew when you might come across a nice straight hazel stick growing in the wood, or a nice beech tree to carve your initials on. Often on his way home from school a young lad would loup the fence into a field of growing turnips (particularly Swedes) and pull one up. The knife was needed to cut off the shaws and roots. A succulent, juicy young neep took a lot of beating!

On frosty mornin's fit I dread
Is stannin' in a caal' cairt shed
Fin roon' the neuk the foreman creeps
"Jist you ging an' pu' some neeps."

They're witin' there in lang stracht raa's
Ma hacket han's grip frozen shaa's
I see it fin I ging tae sleep
A muckle sonsie Sweddish neep.

Bit hiv ye tried een fresh an' raa' ?
There's naething tae compare at a'.
Yer funcy aipples you can keep,
I'd raether taste a juicy neep.

THE SECRET LAND

By Amy Thomson aged 10, Northmuir Primary School, Kirriemuir.

Each year, the Rotary Club of Kirriemuir runs an essay competition for the 8 or so primary schools in the area. There are prize winners for each class, P1 through to P7 and also a prize for the overall winner of all the schools. In 2010 the overall winner was my granddaughter Amy and I am very pleased to include Amy's story in this book.

Once upon a time there was a beautiful young girl called Amelia. Amelia had long and flowing blonde hair, baby blue eyes and a smile that could light up the world. The deep dark forest of Dean was her home. When she was five years old she had been abandoned there. There was a small area of grass and a cold stream and that was where Amelia had lived for eleven years.

One normal Saturday morning Amelia was just going for a walk along the edge of the stream when suddenly a puff of glitter came from one of the rocks under a waterfall. Amelia ran to see what it was. When she got there, one of the rocks was shining like a bright light. Amelia just touched it gently and it turned into a pathway into the waterfall. In the distance a bright gold light was shining. Amelia was apprehensive but she still went along the path to the light. The light suddenly disappeared and Amelia was left in the dark, cold and gloomy tunnel. She closed her eyes tightly and then opened them with a jerk. All around was filled with fairies and magical creatures. She could not believe it. She was in a different land.

A small, pretty fairy came up to Amelia and asked, "Are you lost young child?" "Yes, I appear to be in a different land," Amelia replied. Suddenly, the fairy flew off. Amelia followed her with difficulty. After a few minutes Amelia got too tired and sank down on the ground into a heap of leaves. Amelia fell into a deep sleep. When Amelia woke up she was having a bath in human stew! Amelia looked around and she saw a massive bogie green, lumpy, fat and scary troll. The troll spotted her looking at him and he bounded over to her. "My name is Hogisbogis," the troll boomed. "Mmm...Mmm My name is Amelia. Please don't eat me, Hogisbogis." "I shall eat you if I want to," boomed Hogisbogis.

Hogisbogis started tipping carrots, onions and tomatoes in with Amelia. Suddenly, Hogisbogis gave out a loud yell because a man had stuck a sword in his leg. "I am Prince Lagoon and I am here to slay you foul beast and save the fair maiden." Prince Lagoon threw a rope around Hogisbogis's neck and pulled him to the ground. Then he stuck his sword in Hogisbogis's eye killing him for good. Next, Prince Lagoon threw a rope into the pot and pulled Amelia out. Then he said in a kind voice, "Hold on to me," and he orbed her out.

They arrived in a beautiful palace and Amelia asked Prince Lagoon what he had just done. Prince Lagoon replied, "I orbed you out. It means I used magic to transport you out of there." Amelia then looked at Prince Lagoon for the first time and she immediately fell in love with him. He was a tall prince with dark brown hair, hazel eyes and a truthful smile. It was strange because at that very same moment Prince Lagoon had also fallen in love with Amelia. They looked into each other's eyes and knew that it was meant to be. Prince Lagoon took Amelia to a ring of fairy toad stools and proposed to her. Amelia said "Yes" straight away and they got married that day.

The marriage ceremony was in a beautiful golden cathedral with amazing art work covering the walls. Prince Lagoon was dressed in a white suit with his sword and many medals and Amelia was dressed in a gorgeous white lace and silk wedding dress, a fluttering white veil, a flowing white silk train and a diamond encrusted tiara.

Many magical creatures came to the wedding of Prince Lagoon and Amelia. The ceremony brought a tear to the eye. In fact it was so emotional that even Prince Lagoon (who was known for his bravery) had to hold back a tear. After the wedding there was a massive party with food, wine and dancing. Prince Lagoon and now Princess Amelia received thousands of wedding gifts but the most special of all was the spell that gave Prince Lagoon and Princess Amelia a child. The child was a baby boy that they named Leo. Prince Lagoon, Princess Amelia and baby Leo all lived happily ever after.

MURRAY THE PUDDOCK

When I was at primary school in the 1950's it was quite common (for the boys anyway) to call one another by nicknames. The nicknames given were many and varied and in today's society some of them would not be tolerated, for example, "Fatty", "Specky", and so on. I can't imagine what Mr. & Mrs. Buttar were thinking about when they named their son Roland! His nickname was "The Bap". Compared to some, I was quite lucky because my nickname, "Tamsen" was just a derivative of my Thomson surname - others were not quite so fortunate. One boy was called "Murray the Puddock". This child's round face resembled a frog's not least because he wore thick glasses which magnified his eyes. Matters were not helped by his parents dressing him in a green jacket with matching trousers!

Murray the puddock wis juist a young loon
His een they bulged oot an his face it wis roon.
He wore a green jacket wi briks made tae match
Fin he louped aboot he wis richt hard tae catch.

At the skweel sports he won ilky race
High jump or relay The Puddock wis ace.
His gangly legs were lang an gie thin
But fair did the job fin he needit tae rin.

Noo Murray's grown up an he's teen a lass
A bonny young quine that he thinks is first class.
There's a new bairnie due juist ony day noo
Fin the tadpole appears wull Murray get fu' ?

THE CAAL

Oh! Goad Almichty fit's adee
I've a stappit nose an wattery ee
My throat's as if I've swalliet preens
There's aches 'n pains in a' ma beens

I sneeze like I've been snuffin' spice
An' a puddock's croak is noo ma v'ice
Ma hackin' hoast near gars ma greet
An every hunkie's soaken weet

I've aiten peels baith fite an' blue
Eneuch tae gar a body spue
Pooders an' toddies, I've tried 'em a'
Bit ma caal's still here - nae slack ava

I'm walkin' like a half shut knife
An' seeken' solace fae the wife
Bit my peer plight she's nae for seein'
I jist get tellt I'm far fae deein'

A COUNTRY WENCH

Dark hair and eyes with sultry look
She giggles like a babbling brook.
To secret bower she bids him follow
Her ample bosoms there to wallow.

Who is this creature so devine
That's kindled dormant feelings fine
And stirred within a chaste young youth
Desires unknown till now forsooth.

He'll ne'er forget that lustful hour
Or pleasures learnt in that sweet bower
But will hanker long for the heady stench
Of that sensual earthy country wench.

136

SEAGULLS AIGGS

Not so long ago those living at or near the northeast coast would routinely gather seagulls eggs to supplement their diet. This took place in April and May. On the Buchan coast it was mostly the eggs of the Herring Gull that were collected and eaten although the eggs of the Black Headed Gull were also taken. Herring Gull eggs are olive green with black speckles and are about twice the size of a hen's egg. They are extremely nutritious with rich orange yolks and the "white" has a bluish tinge. In the 1920's and 30's there was quite a trade in collecting gulls eggs which were then sent off to London where they were considered a delicacy and eaten along with champagne. To this day, gulls eggs are popular and in southern restaurants sell for around £4.50 each. One London restaurant recently had gulls egg omelettes with lobster on the menu at £90!

Another source of food from the north sea was dilse (dulse). Dulse seaweed is an edible alga that grows widely along the shorelines of the North Sea and has been picked as a food for thousands of years. It is a good source of iron and is eaten raw. However, a popular way to eat it in Buchan was to part roast it using a pair of flat toed tongs that had been heated red hot. The fresh wet dulse was then squeezed several times with the tongs making it pop and squeak.
The end result was very tasty.

A blue Mye sky an saa't sea air
Fae the tap o' a Buchan Heugh
The cry o' seagulls heich abeen
Gyangs far on the win's saft sough.

Ben the narra twisted roadies
That oor fadders trod afore
Gaithered aiggs fae nests on granite
Richt doon tae the rocky shore.

Syne pu'ed some sa'ty shiny dilse
For roasten wi the tyangs
An' suppered weel on fresh gulls aiggs
That put flicht tae hunger's pangs.

THE SHORTEST DAY

Dreary mornin's dark an weet
Daylicht 'oors a welcome treat.
It's efter acht afore it's licht
On winter mornin's dark as nicht.

Syne the solstice comes at last
Mid sleaty dribbles or snavvy blast.
An' efterneen has near begun
Afore there's ony hint o' sun.

Maist days it's nivver seen ava
Wi leaden cloods that threaten sna'.
On caal dank days wi' heavy shower
It's dark again afore it's fower.

Bit langer days they will appear
A wik or twa in the new 'ear.
A little faarer ilky day
A henny's stride as aal folk say.

An' fin ye add them a thegidder
It a' maks up for lichter widder
The days are stretchin' say the folk
It'll seen be time tae shift the clock.

THE TURRA COO

In 1911 the then Chancellor of the Exchequer LLoyd-George introduced the National Insurance Act. This required employers to pay contributions for their employees to enable the employees to obtain some monetary benefit when they were off sick. This legislation was unpopular with employers and in particular an Aberdeenshire farmer named Robert Paterson who farmed at Lendrum Farm near Turriff. Paterson was not happy at being forced to pay the National Insurance levy as it was his opinion that country people were hardier than their city counterparts who worked in unhealthy factories - and in any case, it was Paterson's position that he had always looked after his workers when they were ill and so he refused to pay. In 1913 he was taken to court and fined and again refused to pay the fine. A sheriff then decided that the court would seize goods from Paterson and that they be sold to pay the fine. Paterson's white milk cow was impounded and brought to the square in Turriff to be sold. However, a large crowd gathered in support of Paterson and a riot ensued and the cow escaped but only to be taken to the mart in Aberdeen where local farmers rallied round and bought it. The cow was then taken home to Lendrum Farm where it enjoyed its celebrity status for a further six years before it eventually died. Thereafter, the story of the "Turra Coo" became folklore as successive generations of country bairns learned of the tale from their parents and grandparents. A statue of the Turra Coo is due to be erected in Turriff in 2010.

The Turra coo wis teen fae hame
A victim o' a high powered game
Bit a fite haired mannie fae London toon
Wis nae a match for a fairmer loon.

He tried tae gar him pey a deal
For cotter lads that were nae weel
But Lendrum said, "Jist ging tae hell,
Ma cottars I'll tak' care masel."

Lloyd Geordie he wis nae neen pleased
Bit a Sheriff's rule his ire had eased.
We'll gar the fairmer pey the noo
For we'll jist sell his aal' fite coo.

Fin Turra folk heard o' the plan
They up in airms each till a man.
Their wifies tee took tae the streets
An' followin' on wis a' their geets.

The coo wis tethered in the square
Wi' lots o' folk a' stannin' there.
Bids were socht fae a sheriff's man
An' a riot syne got oot o' haan'.

Eggs an' neeps flew throwe the air
An' the sheriff's man wis hurtet sair.
Bit he ran for hame at the final deed
Wi a chunty pot teem't ower 'is heid.

Tae Aiberdeen the coo it went
Bocht but syne tae hame wis sent.
At Lendrum fairm it spent its days
It's famous state it didna faze.

Noo a hunner 'ears has near gaen by
An' Turra folk still like their kye.
So if ye ging tae that toon noo
Ye'll see a statue for their coo.

FIFTEEN SIXTY NINE

In the 1940's and 50's and before most people had cars, country dwellers relied on the various delivery vans for their groceries, butcher meat, fish and drapery items. In those days many people shopped at the Co-operative Society and bought their groceries and butcher meat from the vans that called on a weekly basis. The attraction of being a "Co-opy" member was that for every £1 spent you got a "dividend" which you could cash in when it suited. Co-opy members all had their "divvy" numbers and as a small child I often stood at the van whilst my mother get her messages. For some reason, her divvy number sticks in my mind to this day!

The Co-opy had a puckle vans
That trailed the country roon'.
Bakers eens an' butchers eens
That cam' oot fae the toon.

They stottet up the steeny road
That led tae mither's craft
Wi crusty loaf an Paris buns
An' rowies fine an' saft.

The butcher he had sassages
An' pun's o' mince sae reid.
Fine stewin' steak an' bilin' beef
That made the broth taste gweed.

Syne wi' the eerins totted up
He ticked the message line,
"Noo fits yer divvy number lass?"
"It's Fifteen Sixty Nine".

FEELINGS

A caring smile and friendly word
Can move someone to tears
But angry words with little thought
Can hurt for countless years.

So take a while before you speak
Your broadside to let go.
For one you love may well be hurt
Much more than you will know.

TWA HUNTER LADS

Twa hunter lads cam' creepin' throwe,
Creepin' throwe the wuid.
An' they hae killed twa rabbits,
Which they kent wis forbid.

Twa hunter lads cam' creepin' throwe,
Creepin' throwe the wuid.
An' they hae killed a big brown hare,
An' baith drank o' its bluid.

Twa hunter lads cam' creepin' throwe,
Creepin' throwe the wuid.
An' they hae killed a mither goat
An' taen awa' her kid.

Twa hunter lads cam' creepin' throwe,
Creepin' throwe the wuid.
An' they hae killed a black haired boar,
Because they thocht they shuid.

Twa hunter lads cam' creepin' throwe,
Creepin' throwe the wuid.
An' they hae killed a fine young stag,
An' the gralloch they hae hid.

Twa hunter lads cam' creepin' throwe,
Creepin throwe the wuid.
An' they hae killed her ladyship,
Because the Laird had bid.

Twa hunter lads cam' creepin' throwe,
Creepin' throwe the wuid.
An' the Laird's new wife has slain them baith
For she kens what they did.

HIPPENS

Washing machines, tumble driers and busy working Mums have
seen the demise of terry nappies and drastically altered the content
of many washing lines.

Far hiv a' the hippens geen
That eased tae wave on the dryin' green?
Ye'd see them hingin' in a raa'
Bonny, clean an' fite as snaa'.

Hippens they could tell a lot.
If a wife wis clean or not.
For claiken neebours seen wid say,
"She pits oot washin' that is grey."

New dads affen lost their cool
Fin left tae change een that wis fule.
Their cries were heard in ilky room
As the safety preen did brob their thoom'.

Each hippen hid tae be jist richt,
It wis nae ease if it wis ticht.
Bit then again, ower slack wis wau'r,
For the leakin' stuff wid traivel far!

Yon modern quines hinna' lived at a'
Wi' nappies that they throw awa'.
Wi' a line o' hippens it wis affa' clear,
It's a little bairn that bides in here!

LOUPIE FOR LOUP

When my sons were little their grandad would take them in turn on his knee and recite this old Buchan ditty. All the while, he held their ankles which were moved in a circular motion as if riding a horse. At the third line, the child's right foot was tapped on the left foot then at the fourth line, the left foot was tapped on the right foot.   The process was repeated for lines five and six. The galloping motion was then speeded up as fast as could be for the last two lines and invariably the toddler would laugh and giggle and shout, "Again, again."   I had forgotten about this old rhyme until my own grandchildren came along and true to form, they also demanded, "Again, again." after the verse was recited.I suspect that the verse is quite old but who the author was I have no idea.

> This is the doggies that gaed tae mill dam
> Loupie for loup an' loupie for spam.
> Wi' a lick oot o' this mullart's meal pyoke
> An' a drink oot o' that mullart's mill dam
> Wi' a lick oot o' this mullart's meal pyoke
> An' a drink oot o' that mullart's mill dam.
> Syne loupie for spam an' loupie for spam
> An' hame an' hame an' hame an' hame.

CHRISTMAS DAY

I well remember Christmas Day, 1949. That was the year my little sister and I didn't get any toys! I was four years old and we had just flitted down to Perthshire from Aberdeenshire in November. At that time, in the area of Buchan where we lived Christmas was just another day and was not celebrated. Country bairns all got their toys on New Year's Day which was a holiday. My parents hadn't realised that customs in Perthshire were different. Now we certainly did get our toys that year but I can't remember if it was on Boxing Day or if we had to wait until New Year's Day but I recall my mother explaining that with so many children in the world, Santa Clause couldn't deliver all the gifts in one night and had to come round a second time! The next year and every year thereafter we got our toys on Christmas Day like everyone else.

Huddlet roon' a roarin' fire
It is a hamely sicht.
Three little fair haired bairnies,
Their een a' shinin' bricht.

Ootside the wintry win' does blaa'
It rattles the stable door.
The sna' blaa's intae muckle wreathes
That wid gar a body smore.

But safe inside their cosy hoose
The bairnies lach an' play.
They wunna' sleep a wink the nicht
For the morn is Christmas Day.

WIR LUM'S UP

With most people now having gas or oil central heating, chimney fires are a rarity, but fifty years or so ago they were quite common when the population relied on coal, logs or peat to heat their houses. At that time it was essential to have the chimney swept once a year and this was done either by calling in a local chimney sweep or in many country areas, householders would have their own set of brushes and do the job themselves. Soot from the fire would gradually build up inside the chimney and a wayward spark was often all that was required to ignite the soot causing a chimney fire. When this happened, clouds of acrid black sooty smoke would billow out from the chimney pot and frequently sparks and flames would shoot out as well. Inside the house, the noise of a chimney fire could be quite scary. It roared somewhat like the wind during a stormy gale. In addition, smoke would sometimes billow out from the hearth and chunks of smouldering soot would fall down the chimney and roll out over the floor. Most chimney fires, although frightening at the time, burned themselves out within ten or fifteen minutes. In Scotland, if you lived within a "burgh", i.e. a city or small town you came under the jurisdiction of the Burgh Police (Scotland) Act, 1892. Under this legislation it was an offence to let your chimney go on fire and if you did, the Fire Brigade would attend and the police would charge you. You were then summoned to the Burgh Court where the going rate for a chimney fire was a fine of 10 shillings (50 pence). Thus you had a criminal record!

Yoamin rik as black as nicht
It nips yer een an' dulls yer sicht.
Ye hoast an' cowk yer plight is dire,
Oh michty me, wir lum's on fire.

Up in the reef ye hear it roar
Ye maun get oot or else ye'll smore
But bleezin shunners tummel doon
An' sitty rik it swirls aroon'.

In twinty meenits it's a' brunt oot
Naething left bit the smell o' soot.
The hoose inside's an affa sicht
Ilky thing will need a dicht.

Tae pey a sweep it can be dear
But ye'll no' need him until next 'ear.
So steady noo wi sticks or coal
Anither fire ye canna thole.

THAT'S NAETHING

A lad that I ken has aye deen it a'
Fitivver I've deen, he's deen it times twa.
If I've geen ti the hulls an' walk't for miles,
" That's naething." says he, "I've walk't tae the Isles."

His gairden's aye better nur abody else,
Wi muck fae the byre he's mixed wi some dilse.
"Foo big's yer carrots?" he speirs wi a smirk.
" That's naething." says he, "Mine chocket a stirk."

On Setterday nicht he's aye at the dance,
Wi a mannie like him there's neen has a chance.
There's a lass on ma airm, so I say, "I'm awa'."
" That's naething." says he, "I'm takin' hame twa'."

I tell't him ae day o' a lad that I ken,
That has as much sense as the teeth o' a hen.
An' forbye that as weel, he's gie prone tae blaa'
" That's naething." says he, "I ken him an' a'."

A SKEIN O' GEESE

"Cord number one," said the undertaker and Albert Forbes stepped forward to the side of the grave. He took the cord from the undertaker and stood head bowed at the head of the coffin. "Cord number two," was cried and forward came Geordie Forbes, Albert's brother. "Number three," said the undertaker and handed this cord to Bill Forbes the youngest of the three brothers. Twenty year old Norman Jamieson could feel his heart thumping loudly in his chest. He was nervous as this was the first funeral he had been to where he had to take an active part. He looked around the silent mourners at his granda's funeral in the little cemetery just outside Strichen and wondered if they too would hear his heart thumping.

Norman's mother Peggie was the eldest of the four Forbes siblings and as eldest grandchild, Norman was given the honour of getting a cord. He was glad that so far, he had endured the stress of the funeral. He had been near to tears inside the little kirk when the minister mentioned that he and granda had been close but with a struggle he had managed to keep his composure although if anyone had spoken to him, he couldn't have replied. "Cord number four," said the undertaker and Norman stepped forward. He had been to several funerals in his young life but this was the first time he had stood so close to the coffin. He looked down at the polished oak lid and read the brass nameplate.

"JAMES FORBES
1867 - 1956"

Norman knew that his granda had been 89 years old but he had never given much thought to the year of his birth and when he saw it on the brass plate it seemed an awful long time ago. As the remaining cords were given out to other family members, young Norman let his mind drift back to the many happy times he had spent with his granda.

Norman, his mother and granda had lived in the little croft of Sunnybrae at the foot of Mormond Hill. Norman couldn't remember much about his father who had been in the Merchant Navy. As such he had travelled the world and was away for months on end as Norman was growing up. His times at home grew less and less until eventually he just stopped coming home altogether. Norman was never particularly close to his dad and the subject of his dad's non-return was never raised in his presence. It was his granda that Norman turned to for a father figure and the pair of them were very close. Granda Forbes was typical of his generation. He was about 5'8" with a ruddy complexion and moustache. He wore a tweed bonnet and usually sported two or three day's stubble as he only shaved on Wednesday and Saturday nights. Norman and he would go for long walks together and discuss the world and its ways. On warm days they would sit outside on the drystane dyke of pink granite that surrounded the garden of the croft. Granda Forbes had removed four or five coping stones from the top and replaced them with an oblong granite slab, just enough for a man and a boy to sit on and it was there that they spent many hours discussing all manner of things.

Their conversations on the dyke usually started with the ritual of granda lighting his pipe. It was a short stubby Stonehaven briar with a silver lid. Granda would take out his old leather sploochan and pull out a length of black bogie roll tobacco. Some tobacco would be cut off which was then sliced into smaller pieces. Granda would then rub the whole lot back and forth in the palms of his hands until he got the tobacco to the required texture. The old burnt ashes would be scraped out, the pipe re-filled then granda would crack a spunk and light his pipe. If it was a windy day, two or three attempts would have to be made and granda would look at his box of Swan Vestas and remark, "Aye, I've been gie hard on the spunks the day." Only when the pipe was successfully lit would the serious business of conversation commence.

150

It was usually Norman who started proceedings by asking a question. "Div ye think there could be folk livin on ither planets Granda?" Granda would take a sook or two at his pipe then a well aimed spit would unerringly hit an old disused stone cheese chessel that sat about four feet out from the dyke. "Weel, there could be laddie, there could be," said Granda. "Ye see we're here, so I dinna see foo there couldna be ither folk somewye else lookin doon on's." "Div ye think that some day folk'll ging tae the meen?" Norman would ask. "Aye maybe they wull," replied Granda. "Bit I doot I'll nivver see't. Bit ye nivver ken. Fin I wis a loon there wis nae cars nor aeroplanes an juist look fit's happenin iv noo." "I wid like tae mak rockets tae flee tae the meen," said Norman. "Oh weel, ye'll need tae stick in at the skweel if ye're gaan tae dee that,"
said Granda.

"Div you mine on the tattie famine? asked Norman. "The fit laddie?" asked Granda. "The tattie famine," repeated Norman. "Miss Rodgers tellt's that lang ago a' the folk in Ireland wis hungert tae death." "Na faith ye loon, I'm nae as aal's a' that," laughed Granda. "Bit my grandfadder easst tae tell's aboot it. It happened in aichteen forty six. The folk in Ireland grew an affa lot o' tatties an that wis a' they lived on ilky day. Syne the tattie blight got in amon the crap an rotted em so the peer folk juist stairved kis they'd naething else tae ate. Some o' them cam ower tae Scotland at at time." "Fit wis tattie blight?" enquired Norman. "It wis a disease that gaed in amon the tatties and juist rotted them. They a' gaed wrang an didnae lest throwe the winter so the peer folk juist stairved tae death," said Granda. "Did it nae come tae Scotland?" queried Norman. "Aye laddie, it cam here as weel," said Granda. "In fact it's still here yet. Ye see at dreel o' Duke o' Yorks owere ere," said granda, indicating potatoes growing in his garden and sending another well aimed spit at the chessel. "Ye'll see that een or twa stems at the en o' the dreel hiv turned gie yalla. Weel I widna be surprised if at's blight. We hid gie damp mochie wither at the start o' the simmer an at's the kine o' wither that blight thrives on." "Did a lot o' folk in Scotland dee o' hunger?" asked Norman. "Some did," said Granda. "Bit nae as muckle as in Ireland. Ye see the folk in Ireland ate maistly tatties an naething else bit it wis different here. In Scotland until nae affa lang ago it wis oat meal that folk maistly ate tho' they ate tatties as weel. Fin ye were fee'd at a place ye got sae muckle steen o'meal, eneuch for yer sax month fee. I aye mine, fin I wis thirteen an gaed tae ma first fee at Mains o' Watterton, I files got meal three times a day."

"Meal three times a day?" said Norman with incredulity. "Aye, laddie, three times a day," said Granda. Ye see, Watterton wis a gie hungry aal bugger so I got brose for ma brakfist, syne twa meallie jimmies at dennir time an syne a plate o' milk porritch at nicht." "Oh surely no, " said Norman. "At's a fact ma loon, things were gie hard at at time, bit files on a Sunday I got a bilte eggie," said Granda with a wink. Norman did not know whether to believe him or not.

Then as often was the case, Norman would dramatically change the subject. Fit div ye think happens till ye fin ye're deid Granda?" Div ye ging somewye else?" "Michty laddie, at's some affa stuff that ye're speirin at's the day. I juist dinna ken fit happens fin ye're deid, bit at ten 'ear aal, yer far ower young tae be worrying aboot things like at," said Granda. "Miss Rodgers says that if ye're coorse ye ging tae hell but if ye're gweed an weel behaved ye ging tae hivven," said Norman. "Weel at's fit some folk say," said Granda. "Bit there's naebody kens tho' there's ither's that believes in reincarnation." "Fits reincar... reincar... at thing that ye said. Fit's at?" said Norman. "Weel," said Granda. "Some folk think that efter yer deid, ye come back as somebody or something else." "Ach, ye're hae'in ma on Granda." said Norman unbelievingly. "No, I'm nae at laddie, some folk think that they'll come back later on as some idder body." "Could they maybe come back as a dog or a beast?" asked Norman. "Some think they can." said Granda." "I'd like tae come back as a lion."

said Norman letting out a roar. "On the ither han," said Granda with a sly grin, "Ye mith come back as a gollach an syne somebody mith trump on ye." The pair of them laughed at the thought. "Fit wid you like tae come back as Granda?" asked Norman. "A weel, at's for me tae ken an for you tae fin oot ma loon," said granda, not very forthcoming.

Norman noticed that during their conversation his Granda was always looking skyward as if searching for something. "Fit are ye lookin for Granda," queried Norman. "I'm lookin for ma aal freens," said granda. "They're due ony day noo." "Fitna freens?" asked Norman rather puzzled. "The geese laddie, the geese, said Granda." They come ilky 'ear withoot fail, aye aboot the 17th. o' September. They flee richt ower abeen the hoose an say hullo tulls. Some 'ears they're a day or twa early an some 'ears they're a day or twa late bit iss is the seventeenth an I've been lookin oot for them for a day or twa." "Far div they come fae?" asked Norman. "I'm nae richt sure." said Granda. "It's aither Canada or Greenland, bit its gie far awa onywye." "Foo div they ken far tae come tull?" asked Norman. "There's naebody kens at," said Granda. "They've been comin tae the same place for hunners or maybe thoosans o' 'ears, bit foo they manage it, I dinna ken." Just then a faint cackle could be heard in the sky and Granda pointed excitedly towards the sea. "Here they come laddie, here they come." Norman noticed three large skeins of geese flying high in "V" formations. They flew directly over the croft cackling as they went heading inland. Granda stood up and waved to them. "See," said Granda, "I tell't ye they'd say hullo tulls. They'll be makkin for Strathbeg Loch for the winter." "Fan div they ging hame?" asked Norman. "April or Mye fin the wither's better," said Granda.

"Lift and gently lower," said the undertaker bringing Norman quickly back to reality. He let the smooth gold coloured cord slip through his fingers until the coffin came to rest at the bottom of the grave. Then following the others, he let the cord drop and watched it hit the coffin lid with a thump. He looked down into the grave and was surprised at how deep it was . He knew it would be about six feet but it seemed an awful lot deeper than that looking down from above.

A few weeks after the funeral Norman went back to University where he started the third year of a four year maths and physics course. On leaving university he obtained employment with an aeronautical firm in England and would return to Scotland to visit his mother at Sunnybrae twice or three times a year. Always when he came back he would visit his granda's grave in the little cemetery on the hill but strangely enough, he never really felt close to him there. The only place where he felt his granda's presence was when he sat on the garden dyke at Sunnybrae where the two of them had spent so many carefree hours. On these visits, Norman would sit on the granite slab alone with his thoughts and smile to himself as he recollected their conversations of long ago. He would sometimes try and emulate his granda by spitting at the old chessel but that was a trick he could never master as the spittle usually just ran down his chin.

Norman's career in maths and physics took off and he eventually obtained an important post in America working for N.A.S.A. on satellite guidance systems. He married an American girl and they had a son James Forbes Jamieson named after his grandfather. Norman, his wife and son came home to Scotland for a holiday in September of 1978 when young James was aged seven. Norman delighted in showing his family where he was brought up, the school he had gone to and also the little croft where he had lived all of his young life with his mother and grandfather. By this time his mother had died and the croft was unoccupied and in disrepair. The garden was overgrown but the granite dyke was still there as was the old stone chessel. Norman and young James sat on the granite slab on the dyke as Norman told his son about his granda and the conversations they had once had there.

As they were talking, a faint cackle could be heard coming in from the sea. "Look James, here come the geese." said Norman. A large "V" shaped skein winged their way directly overhead. They had almost passed when a single solitary goose broke off from the formation and flew round the old croft a couple of times before carrying on to rejoin the skein. Norman rose to his feet and waved. It was at that moment he felt the overwhelming presence of his granda far stronger than he had ever done since his death. "Why did that one do that dad?" asked James. Norman's eyes misted over as he put his arm round his son's shoulder and whispered, "It was just an old friend saying hullo."

KITTLINS

An essential element of the livestock of any farm is cats. In addition to the farmer's wife's "house" cat and any kept by cottars as pets, most farms had 2 or three who were necessary to keep down rats and mice. These "farm" cats were hunters and slept in the byre or barn and would be given a bowl of milk after milking time. Sometimes they would get a treat of "saps" i.e. bits of bread broken up and steeped in the milk. The farmer was often part of a long generation of his family who had lived and worked on the same farm. So too the farm cats. They would come from a long line of previous generations mostly descended through the female line that were connected to that particular location. Of course from time to time, after a visit from a roving tom, the cats gave birth to kittens. These were usually dispatched after a few days. They were put in a sack weighted by a stone and then immersed in a pail of water and drowned. It was only very occasionally that a kitten would be reprieved, perhaps if one of the resident cats was getting old or if the kitten had particularly attractive markings, tortoise shell for example, would it escape. Thus, the ritual drowning kept the cat population to an acceptable level. I have no doubt that such practices still go on but in today's climate would be frowned upon. However, a generation or so ago no one gave much thought to it. At a time when human infant mortality was much higher than today, for those who lived and worked on the land the despatching of a few kittens was neither here nor there.

Trixie's paddin' back an' fore
An' listens tae ilky soun'
She's lookin for 'er kittlins
They've been teen awa' tae droon.

She hid them weel awa fae us
An' kept them oot o' sicht
Bit their meowin' gave the game awa'
In the riggin' o' the nicht.

Seyvin kittlins in a nest
At the en' o' the stable laft
Een ticht shut an' cuddlet doon
Amang the hye sae saft.

Syne picket up an' seckit
Wi a muckle steen sae caal
An' plunket in the milkhoose pail
Wi' watter fae the waall.

Trixie's paddin' back an' fore
She's listened tae ilky soond.
Her kittlins they've been teen awa'
An' ilky een's been drooned.

MEH DUNDEE DOAG

I had never set foot in Dundee until I was about 17 and then only
intermittently after that.   However, in 1974 I went to work there
for a few years.   During my time in Dundee I got to know a lot
of people.   Dundonians are warm hearted and homely with a great
sense of humour.   I was fascinated by their accents - particularly
of the older people.   This poem is just a wee bit of nonsense
"strait aff the tap o' meh heid."

Meh wee doag's a bra' wee doag
It gaes tae the shoap itsel'
He brings me back meh paypir
An' a packet o' fags as well

He sleeps oan 'is back wi's belly turned up
An' he gies 'is tail a flick
'Is tongue comes oot when he wakin's up
An' he gies 'is pa's a lick

He growls an barks when the visitors come
Even tho' it's jist oor Betty
Then he'll run ootside and hae a snuff
An' pee through the rails o' wir plettie

Meh wee doag's a mongrel doag
A pedigree's no' for me
For he's the best doag in a' the toon
Fae Fintry tae Lochee.

HOGMANAY

Aince mair yer stealthy creep I feel
Anither year o' mine ye steal.
As starin at the dying flame
I wonder whar this last year's gane.

On lookin' back I cast my e'e
An' think o' freen's nae mair I'll see.
O' kindly words I should have said
But now too late for they are dead.

Or childhood days withoot a care
Oh how I wish tae be back there.
But bygane days we shouldnae mourn
For ithers now must get their turn.

An' as the auld year slips awa'
There's sadness an' a tear or twa.
But then oor spirits upward lift
A fresh New Year oh what a gift.

We'll think nae mair o' auld lang syne
For yesterdays we shouldnae pine.
Wi' lichtsome he'rt and conscience clear
We'll mak' the best o' this New Year.

ANOTHER TIME AND PLACE

The late Scottish playwright, Jessie Kesson was born Jessie Grant McDonald in 1916 in Inverness. Jessie and her unmarried mother moved to Elgin where they lived in extreme poverty. In 1934 Jessie got married to John Kesson. Her literary career took off after she started contributing to the Scots Magazine. Thereafter she wrote plays for the BBC. In 1947 she moved to London and went on to produce "Women's Hour" on BBC Radio. Her plays include "Where the Apple Ripens", "The White Bird Passes" and "Another Time, Another Place." Although I have never read the latter play, its name intrigued me and was the inspiration for this poem. Jessie Kesson died in 1994.

Her voice was like the nightingale
At the end of a perfect day
A sweeter sound he ne'er would hear
Until his dying day.

Oh he could love that bonny lass
Though he knew that could not be
For he must lead another life
And the same it was for she.

But oft alone on summer walks
He saw her smiling face
And dreamed of things that might have been
In another time and place.

SHAKKINS 'EE PYOKE

The "shakkin's 'ee pyoke" is a rural expression meaning the remainder or the last remnants. It stems from a time when grain, particularly oats (corn) was kept in jute sacks. Each grain of corn has a little hook at its end and there is a tendency for the grains to cling onto the inside of a sack when emptied - and as generations of farm youngsters know if you ran through a pile of corn in the granary you ended up with a whole lot of corn grains clinging to your socks!. To properly empty a sack of oats you had to give it a good shake after the bulk of the contents had been poured out. And so the phrase "shakkins 'ee pyoke" simply came to mean the last drop of anything at all. This poem therefore is the "shakkins o' my pyoke!

Davy Smith had thirteen geets,
His cooncil hoose took up twa streets.
Een on ae side, syne anither
Roon' 'i neuk fae his aal' mither.

His neebours at him aye wis quizzen',
"Wid he increase his baker's dizzen?"
Said Davy, "Na, an' 'at's nae joke,
For 'at's 'i shakkin's o' ma pyoke."

THE HENS' POT

A generation or so ago most people living on farms kept a dozen or so hens. These could be free range i.e. allowed to roam free round the farmyard returning each night to be shut into a henhouse. Otherwise they would be kept in a henrun - a netting wire enclosure, oblong in shape perhaps about 10 or 12 yards long and about four or five yards wide. The henrun also contained the henhouse. The disadvantage of free range hens was that they sometimes laid away from the henhouse in stackyards or at the bottom of a hedgerow and in such cases unless the nest was found quickly, the eggs were lost. The supply of fresh eggs was important to a country family for food and also for baking. Any extra eggs would be sold to supplement relatively low agricultural wages Hens were fed with bruised corn (oats that had been passed through a machine called a "bruiser" which crushed and flattened them) and any other table scraps that were available. Most men employed on farms had, in addition to their wages, their perks, i.e. free oatmeal, potatoes, milk and feeding for their hens. Scottish winters can be quite harsh and during severe weather instead of the cold bruised corn, the hen's pot would be put on to boil in the late afternoon. This was an old cooking pot that had seen better days and was exclusively used for the hens. The contents would be many and variable - bruised corn, water, potato peelings and any other available scraps. After boiling for an hour or so the contents would be sprinkled with red Carswood Spice (a mixture of spices added to the feed to keep hens on the lay) then "mashed" with a "tattie chapper" (potato masher) and then fed to the hens giving them an eagerly awaited hot feed on a cold winter's day. For hungry children arriving home from school, the tasty aroma emanating from the hens' pot gave them an appetite for their own tea!

Fin winter days were dark an' caal'
Wi' winn'y rain or sleet
Ma mither's hennies a turned oot
they kint they'd get a treat.

For hotterin' on the het peat fire
There wis an aal' roon' pot
Its dents an' brook were testament
It hid been used a lot

Tattie pairin's they gaed in
An' scraps o' loaf as weel
A gowpen fu' o' fine bruised corn
Made up the tasty meal

For chilpin chuckins in a run
Some Carswood spice sae hot
Oh sic a tasty smell it hid
Ma mither's aal' hens' pot.

WULLIE'S APPENDIX.

"At's it settled an," said Margaret Buchan to her father Wullie Robertson. "Ye'll juist come tae bide wi me an Sandy an at'll mak things an affa lot easier for's." "Ah weel, if it'll help ye oot, I suppose I could dee that," said her father.

Wullie had just been conned but didn't realise it. He had lived in his little cottar house at Mains o' Forgue for over fifty years and trying to get him to move out had not been easy. At 87 years old,Wullie was beginning to get a bit forgetful and twice during the last few weeks he had nearly set the place on fire when he left pots on his cooker and had then gone outside and became engrossed in some task or other completely forgetting about the pots until the smoke had billowed out of the back door.

His daughter Margaret and her husband Sandy lived two miles away in the little village of Seggieden just outside Fraserburgh. Margaret was a Principal Teacher of English at Fraserburgh High School and Sandy had a good position with the Planning Department of Aberdeenshire Council. They lived a comfortable life in a three bedroomed bungalow which they had bought from new after selling their previous property some five years earlier. Their two children, Bill and Sally had flown the nest in the last couple of years and were now living with their respective partners in Aberdeen. After the children had left, life for Margaret and Sandy had been easier with more time to themselves but recently she had to help more and more with looking after her dad. On top of her full time teaching duties, this became quite time consuming as she went to see him twice a week to collect his washing and bring him some messages as well as doing a bit of house work. After discussion with Sandy, it became clear that the easiest option all round would be for her dad to come and live with them. Sandy was an easy going lad and got on well with his father-in-law so he didn't raise any objections. The fly in the ointment would be old Wullie himself who was set in his ways and could be a bit crabbit and thraan if things weren't going to his liking.

Margaret knew that if she just sprung the idea of a move on him he would just refuse. She also knew that if she mentioned that he should come to live with her because he was not as able as he once was and was getting forgetful he would deny it and his position would then become entrenched and they would have great difficulty persuading him. After considering things, Margaret used a bit of subterfuge. She started dropping hints to her dad that coming out to help him twice a week was getting a bit beyond her what with her school work and looking after her own house etc. After preparing the ground for a week or two she eventually persuaded him that if he were to move in with them it would be doing her and Sandy a favour and would help her greatly. So honour was satisfied and Willie agreed to the move thinking that he was helping his daughter out by doing her a good turn. There was no mention of his frailties so he did not lose face.

He moved in with Margaret and Sandy in March of 1982. He had his own room with a T.V. and despite the big change in his life, settled in very well with his new routine. He helped Sandy with his garden which was fairly big and would go for walks round the village and meet and blether with some of the old men many of whom he knew from his long years working at nearby Mains o' Forgue. Margaret too noticed a difference. Not having to go out twice a week to tidy her dad's house or make him pots of soup made life much easier for her.

There were however two areas of potential conflict between father and daughter. The first was Wullie's pipe. Margaret was house proud and made it very clear to her dad that she would not permit him to smoke in the house under any circumstances. Wullie had smoked a pipe for more years than he cared to remember. He liked the thick black bogie roll tobacco and his pipe had a bigger than average bowl which he told folk, "Could dampt near tak a

165

hale unce o' tibacca." He very rarely smoked in the mornings but in the afternoons after he had had his dinner he would go and sit outside weather permitting and sook away to his heart's content. If it was cold or wet he would go into Sandy's garden shed for a smoke. He hardly ever went out during the evening so his afternoon smoke often required his pipe to be filled twice and tended to last all afternoon in an effort to stave off the nicotine craving during the evening. Wullie had tried several times to get Margaret to change her mind and allow him to light up his pipe inside but she would not budge. Her ruling was non-negotiable and that was that. Wullie sulked a while and felt that he was hard done by. He hoped that eventually Margaret would take pity on him and give in but she was not for turning.

The second area of conflict was Wullie's clyes and in particular his lang worsit draars, lang sleeved seemits and his collarless thick striped grey flannel sarks. Margaret had tried on many occasions to get him to modernise his wardrobe but he steadfastly refused. His garments had been made to last and Wullie was thrifty. He told her that he had, "Bocht them fifteen 'ear seen fae Morrison's draper's van an there's naething wrang wi them." Morrison's had been an old fashioned gents outfitters established in the Broch for over a hundred years. However they had gone out of business a few years previously as there was now no demand for the type of clothes that they stocked and such items could no longer be had from anywhere. Wullie continued, " If you can affoord tae throw awa clyes that's nae worn oot then yer ower bluiddy weel aff." Margaret knew that she was up against a brick wall and that his intransigence could well be pay back for him not getting to smoke in the house. However, at her husband's insistance, the lang draars and lang sleeved seemits were never put out on her washing line but dried in her tumble drier. Margaret kidded Sandy on, "Your juist feart the neebors think they're yours."

The stand off regarding Wullie's undergarments lasted week after week and there was no sign of him giving in even although evenings would see him sitting sweating profusely because of the central heating. "Yer hoose is far ower het," he would complain to Margaret. "Weel, ye should tak aff yer waiscuit an jacket," retorted Margaret. However, Wullie was used to a cold cottar house and didn't feel right dressed if he was not wearing his old tweed waistcoat and jacket.

May passed into June and the central heating was turned off but with the warmer weather old Wullie was still uncomfortably hot in the house.
However, Margaret had decided to take unilateral action regarding her dad's clyes and one Saturday morning she visited Marks & Spencers in Aberdeen and made several purchases. In the afternoon whilst her dad was out for his walk and smoke Margaret seized her chance and threw out all his pairs of lang draars, seemits and thick flannel sarks replacing them with the new items.

On Sunday mornings Wullie usually had a longer lie and it could be 8.30 or so before he appeared for breakfast. This particular Sunday, Sandy had disappeared early to the golf course having been warned by Margaret that things were coming to a head regarding her dad's clyes. Just after 8 a.m. Wullie shouted, "Faar's ma clean draars an seemit?" "They're in yer boddem draar." shouted Margaret. A moment elapsed, "They're nae at." shouted back Wullie. "Weel ye'll juist hae tae weer fit's ere." shouted back Margaret. There was silence. She waited for five minutes or so then knocked on Wullie's door and entered. There he was standing in Marks and Spencer red and yellow spotted boxer shorts and a modern vest scowling at himself in the full length wardrobe mirror. She could not help but stifle a laugh on seeing his white as ivory legs that had hardly ever seen the light of day for nearly all of his eighty seven years. "It's nae bluiddy funny." said her dad in feigned annoyance. "Look dad, there's some new short sleeved sarks in yer tap draar," said Margaret. "Try een o' them on an see if ye like it." Wullie tried on the shirt and

Margaret could see that he was impressed with his reflection in the mirror. "Aye, it's nae bad," he admitted grudgingly. Margaret thought to herself, "That was a lot easier than I thought" "Bit mine noo, I'm nae geein up ma waiscuit. I need it for ma pocket watch an pipe," said Wullie. "Nor ma jacket," he added. Margaret didn't argue. Having taken the bold step to throw out her dad's underwear and old flannel shirts and replace them with her purchases from M. & S. she didn't want to push her luck too much beyond the victory she had already achieved.

When Wullie got fully dressed and came through to his breakfast he had a smile on his face and was secretly rather pleased with the way he looked. That afternoon he went for a walk as usual and then sat and smoked his pipe on the garden seat for an hour or so before Margaret called Sandy and him in for their tea. Unusually for Wullie, he left some of his tea uneaten and during the course of the meal Margaret had noticed that her dad was quieter than usual and asked if he was alright. "No I'm nae." said Wullie in some distress. "I've gotten a helluva sair side." He placed his hand on his lower right abdomen and said, "It's bluiddy sair an it's gettin worse." Margaret and Sandy then noticed his pale clammy pallor and short laboured breathing. "Div ye think it could be yer appendix Wullie?" asked Sandy with concern. "Aye it could be," said Wullie. "It's gie sair onywye."

Margaret and Sandy panicked a little. They discussed calling the doctor but then decided that the quickest and best thing to do was to take Wullie in the car to the A. & E. at Foresterhill Infirmary in Aberdeen. On the way into hospital Margaret remarked that it was a blessing Wullie was wearing new boxers and they wouldn't have the embarrassment of doctors seeing his old worsit draars. "Trust a wifie tae think like at fin I could be deein," snapped Wullie. Being just after tea time on a Sunday, the A. & E. Department was quiet when they arrived. Wullie walked in bent almost double with pain and was ushered away to a treatment room by a nurse. Margaret and Sandy waited apprehensively in the reception area.

"What seems to be the trouble with you?" enquired the young doctor. "I think ma appendix is gaan ti burst." said Wullie in some alarm. "Take off your clothes and pop onto the bed and we'll have a look." said the doctor. Wullie thought to himself, "I hope you ken fit yer deein ma loon, ye look gie young tae be a doctor." The doctor noticed right away the large reddened area on Wullie's abdomen. He pressed the area gently with his fingers. "Does that hurt?" he asked. "Aye, a bittie," answered Wullie. "Hmm," said the young doctor.

The door of the reception area opened and in walked the young doctor who approached Margaret and Sandy. They stood up and enquired anxiously in unison "Is it his appendix doctor?" "No," said the doctor with a smile. "It's his meerschaum," and handed Wullie's meerschaum pipe to Sandy. "He keeps it in his waistcoat pocket," explained the doctor. "Goad, it's affa het," said Sandy with some surprise as he felt the heat radiating from the pipe's large bowl. Just then Wullie appeared buttoning up his waistcoat. "It's a' your fullt," he said angrily to Margaret. "If I'd still been weerin ma aal thick clyes iss wid nivver hae happened. 'At thin sark an seemit made ma burn masel."

RURAL WIFIES

Thick tweed skirts an sensible sheen
Weel scrubbed faces as bricht's the meen
Eence a month ye should look oot
For there's Rural wifies gaan aboot.

Lang thick hose o' double ply
Hair in buns on heids held high
Ye darna cross each wifie's path
Or else ye'll feel her affa wrath.

They crouch in neuks tae sup their tay
An spik o' jam they've made that day
Or fit is best tae gar cakes rise
An they arnae feart tae critcise.

But though we tease and hae a laugh
Withoot them we wid be worse aff
For Rural men it must be said
Ilky een is richt weel fed.

SILLER TAE BUY A COO

"*Showdie powdie pair o' blue sheen up the Gallowgate doon the green.*" So went the ditty recited by countless Aberdeen mothers in days gone by as they tried to rock their infants off to sleep. In rural areas, if a toddler had slept overlong and had to be wakened up the mother might say, "*If ye sleep ony langer, ye'll sleep yersel intae train ile*" (oil). When country bairns were put to bed they were often told to "*Sleep for siller tae buy a coo.*" Nowadays, these couthy old sayings have largely disappeared with modern youngsters relating more to T.V.'s *Cbeebies, Bob the Builder* and suchlike - what a pity!

Cuddle doon noo little loon
Ye've hid a busy day
Biggin san' pies in a raa
Wi yer pals ye like tae play.

Bit noo its time for sleepy heids
Tae clim' the creaky stair
Yer face clean dichted wi the cloot
I've kaimed yer tuggy hair.

So cuddle doon amang the claes
It's lang by bedtime noo
Dream o' things ye'll dee the morn
An sleep for siller tae buy a coo.

CLERKHILL

A record of farming hardship near Peterhead during the early 19th. century.

In 1772, my great, great, great, grandfather William Thomson, was born near Dunvegan, Skye. At the time of his birth conditions on the island were very severe. Crops were poor, cattle were dying and there had been huge rent increases for the tenantry. During his Hebridean and Scottish tour of 1772, Thomas Pennant wrote this of the island:-

"The poor are left to providence's care. They prowl like other animals along the shore to pick up limpets and other shell-fish, the casual repasts of hundreds during part of the year in these unhappy islands. Hundreds thus annually drag through the seasons a wretched life and numbers unknown, in all parts of the western highlands fall beneath the pressure, some of hunger, more of the putrid fever the epidemic of the coasts originating from unwholesome food the dire effects of necessity."

We do not know who William's parents were. Thomson is a surname that is strangely out of place on Skye around that time. However, there is mention of a James Thomson and a George Thomson at Dunvegan in 1746. This is contained within a remarkable document drawn up by a minister, John Macleod in 1747 and entitled *"List of Those in the United Parish of Duirinish, Waternish and Arnisort who have not been concerned in the Late Wicked and Unnatural Rebellion. Under the heading "Continuing at Home"* appear the names of the above James and George Thomson who may have been relatives of William. Perhaps one of them was his grandfather.

William grew up and was the tenant of land at Idrigill near Dunvegan. In 1792 his rent was increased from £12 per year to £25 per year which coincided with the expiry of his lease. It is thought that William and his brother Andrew left Skye around Whitsun, 1792 and moved round to the northeast of Scotland where they became carters and fishermen. In 1804 when he was 32 William married Isabella Craig who was 23. At that time William was employed as a farm worker near Peterhead.

In 1812 William and Isabella took over the tenancy of Clerkhill Farm which was situated on the southern outskirts of Peterhead. This farm formed part of the Peterhead Estate which had originally been owned by the Keiths who were Earls Marischal of Scotland. In 1715 the Keiths supported the Stuart cause in the Jacobite rising and following the failure of the rebellion their estates were forfeited by the Crown. In 1728 these lands were sold to the Merchant Maiden Company. This was a company formed by the governors of the Maiden Hospital, Edinburgh and the Company of Merchants of the City of Edinburgh. It was from this company that William Thomson leased his farm which extended to about 78 acres and was known as Middletoun of Clerkhill. His annual rent was £93.

Representatives of the Merchant Maiden Company would visit their holdings periodically and report back. In 1825 they reported:-

"The whole of these lands, farms as well as small possessions are under a very good system of culture and improvement. The tenants appear diligent, industrious and intelligent. The lands in general are clean and in good order. The steading of houses possessed by Thomson is ruinous and inadequate. The Governors might consider whether a small addition might not be made to the said houses for the comfort and accommodation of the tenant and his family."

In 1832 the Merchant Company's representative reported:-

"William Thomson's Farm. - This possession is in very good order

but some additions will shortly be required to the steading. The tenant is an active, industrious, hard working man with a family of nine children who, according to their several abilities are all employed in the labours of the farm and are indeed the only servants the tenant keeps. Thomson complains much that the low prices during the last two seasons have thrown him in arrears with his rent. He has been twenty years in possession having succeeded a liferent tenant who left the farm in very bad order. He has now brought it into good condition and if kept up for a year or two with the aid of lime and manure it would soon repay the tenant. Thomson however, has exhausted all his capital as the committee were informed and feels himself unable without assistance to do full justice to the farm in consequence of which his spirits are much depressed. The factor gives this tenant so high a character for industry and economy that the committee feel disposed to recommend him to the Governors as deserving some encouragement from them and they suggest that instead of a reduction of rent which the poor man asked, he should rather get an allowance of £15 or £20 to purchase lime and manure and that he should be allowed time to pay up his arrears which, if granted, the committee believe will relieve him from much anxiety. His total rent is £96.2/- of which he is in arrear at present £33.13.5d."

After twenty years of hard work William Thomson had succeeded in vastly improving his land. At a time when he should have been showing a profit, a depressed market quickly robbed him of his lifetime's hard earned capital. As a result, he was for the first time in arrears with his rent. How cruel a reward for one who had worked so hard. It is little wonder that his *"Spirits were much depressed."* No doubt he recalled past times on Skye when rents were increased and tenants fell into arrears and pondered the awful prospect of it happening again. Over the next two years conditions continued to deteriorate and in 1834 the Merchant Company's representative reported:-

"A great depression of agricultural produce. All tenants with

very few exceptions have exhausted their means and are without capital. They are dependant solely on their crops and the seasons. William Thomson is a very industrious but very poor tenant. He has done ample justice to the land and is deserving of every encouragement.
He is pressing for a reduction in rent."

These reports make very sombre reading. Consider the sentence, *"They are dependant solely on their crops and the seasons."* The implications are quite clear. The tenants had no capital and had to rely solely on their crops to feed themselves. The crops would be poor because there was no extra money for lime to feed the ground. In a season of bad weather, the crops would be worse still. The people at that time would be existing at starvation level.

The year 1835 saw yet another visitation to the Peterhead Estate by the Merchant Company's representatives. On this occasion they reported:-

"William Thomson at Middletoun of Clerkhill who was particularly noticed by the committee in their report of 1832 still continues in the occupation of his farm and is most anxious to get out of his arrear. Some indulgence must eventually be given this poor man who is most frugal and industrious and does his best. The committee authorised the Factor to give him a loft above his house for the accommodation of his rising family and they would recommend to the Governors to sanction a further allowance being given him for lime and manure to keep up his ground and to be expended at sight of the Factor. His farm is certainly high rented in comparison with some of the others and he is so honest and industrious and has so large a family that the committee feel great regret in recommending any measures for recovering his arrears which would have the effect of removing him from his possession."

William Thomson's rent arrears continued to increase despite his hard work. He died in August, 1838 aged 66 years.

After William Thomson's death, the farm tenancy was taken over by his 21 year old son William, who inherited his father's rent arrears.   In 1841 the Merchant Company's representatives reported:-

"Middletoun of Clerkhill - William Thomson (Son).   This tenant succeeded his father, the late William Thomson, who left a wife and large family in August, 1838.   The case of Thomson and his family has been often before the Governors.   They were industrious and hard working but very poor.   Indeed both he and Morrison (a neighbouring tenant) died at no very advanced age and were supposed to have hastened their premature decay by their over-working themselves on their respective farms. Thomson the son, is in arrears with his rent but like Morrison, it is with the exception of £12 or £13 the arrear of the father and in November, 1838, when the Governors agreed to abate one half of Morrison's arrear, they extended the same indulgence to Thomson though effect does not seem to have been given to it by the Factor. The present rent is £110 but the tenant does not think he will be able to pay more than £100 and it will be for the Governors to determine whether they are to accede to this request.   The case is one nearly of charity and the consideration of which is well calculated to excite the kindly feelings of the Governors.

The farm from the view of which the situation commands and its vicinity to Peterhead, is likely to bring at all times a rent above its intrinsic worth but it should not be forgotten that the possession was in very bad order when the late tenant entered to it and that with its improvements he had a hard struggle and with his wife and a numerous family whom he managed to bring up on it he never failed to excite the compassion of each successive deputation of the Governors.   Several of the children are now past majority and one of the sons is a crofter on the Blackhill

*Farm (Mount Pleasant) and one of the daughters is married to
another crofter.   The son now in charge of the farm maintains his
widowed mother and the rest of the family at home.   They are so
frugal that they never asked a new dwellinghouse to which they
are entitled though it became absolutely necessary to renew the
farm steading in a part of which they now reside although it is
scarcely habitable at times from the smoke of which however, the
poor people never complained.   The committee gave the Factor
instructions to get this remedied.   The committee on the whole
would recommend to the Governors to abate the arrears of this
tenant but this to be on condition that the rent shall continue at
£110 as last restricted.   There is a small croft adjacent to this
farm formerly occupied by James Craig (father-in-law of the late
William Thomson) on a liferent lease at a rent of £3.18/-.   Craig
died in March, 1840 and his croft in terms of Thomson's lease is
now added to his farm for which he will have to pay for crop
1841, an additional rent of £11.4.10d.   It may be further
mentioned that Thomson's arrear at present is £186.11/- whereof
£173.17.10d was incurred during his father's life and one half of
this having been abated by the Governors in November, 1838, the
true amount of his fathers arrear may be held to be £86.18.11d."*

William Thomson's widow, Isabella Craig would not have drawn
much comfort from the Merchant Company's visitation.   Despite
her young son's hard efforts since his father's death his own
arrears in addition to those of his father, although virtually halved,
still amounted to nearly £97 or almost one year's rent.   The future
looked bleak for Isabella and her family.   For over ten years they
had been in arrears with the rent.   She no doubt knew that the
Merchant company would not allow this situation to continue
indefinitely.

In 1843 the Merchant Company's representatives reported:-

*"On the Clerkhill property, the committee still found the family of
William Thomson struggling hard to make up their rent.   The
arrears are reduced but they are still considerable, £62.13.3d.,*

the rent being £121.14.10d. The dwelling house is still very uncomfortable and the committee ordered the ceiling to be lathed and plastered so as to keep out the cold and wet and give the family an additional room. They likewise ordered a new milkhouse the situation to be selected by the tenant."

In 1844, the owner's representatives recommended that a new dwellinghouse be built for the family and estimated the cost of this house to be between £130 and £140. In making this recommendation, they suggested a condition be imposed namely that the factor endeavour to obtain payment of the rent arrears and if none was forthcoming then their recommendation was not to proceed. How Isabella and her family viewed this proposition we can only guess. Her son's hard work had reduced the arrears somewhat but they still owed almost six months rent.

In cold reality, there never was any likelihood of them reducing their arrears to an acceptable level given the situation they were in at that time. The promise of a new dwellinghouse in these circumstances was indeed a very hollow one. No doubt the family did try hard to reduce the arrears in an attempt to obtain more comfortable accommodation and to remove from their shoulders the shame of debt but their efforts were in vain. Indeed rather than their arrears being reduced, they were in fact plunged even deeper into debt. By 1846 the attitude of the Merchant Company had hardened considerably. In that year they reported thus:-

"1846, William Thomson's heirs - Middletoun of Clerkhill. The case of this family has been frequently brought before the Governors. The widow and her son, especially the former, are most desirous to remain but they are very poor and considerably in arrear - upwards of one year's rent. The extent of the farm is a little more than 75 acres and averages at present about £1.12.1d. per acre but the Factor thinks he put a high rent on it originally in consequence of its vicinity to the town and that £1.10.6d. only may

be held to be its agricultural value and this rent the family are willing to give. It appears to the committee however, that unless the arrears shall be paid up or security found for payment of the same at the expiration of one or two years this tenant should be parted with and the committee fear the same rule must be adopted in the case of any other tenants who stand in the same situation as Thomson."

Despite William's efforts over the next year the debts increased and in November, 1847, the Merchant Company's representatives reported:-

"William Thomson's heirs. - As these parties are unable to find security for payment of their arrears, the committee think they must be parted with and the farm advertised."

And so after 35 years the tenancy of Clerkhill Farm was lost. The Merchant Company showed compassion for Isabella Craig however because she was allowed to remain in her home until her death in 1867 aged 86. With the passing of Isabella the family's connection with Clerkhill Farm was severed. We do however have an insight into William Thomson's thoughts of his tenancy penned in 1812 when he wrote the undernoted two verses:-

I've cam' tae a place they ca' Clerkhill
It's in the laich o' Buchan.
I think it wid been a better name
Tae ca' it a heilan ' clachan.

The steadin's deen, the dutches fu'
The drains they are a' chocket.
The lan' is clay an' stiff tae ploo
An' gylies watter locket.

It's aichty acres that I've got
Bit the price it is gie dear.
For ninety three poun' is a lot
Tae pey oot ilky 'ear.

Edinburgh men they come an' stan'
Then set ma yearly rent.
Fit ken they o' Buchan lan'
Or the months o' graft I spent.

For twinty 'ears I've vrocht this soil
For forty poun' arrears
Bit a' I've got for my hard toil
Is juist eviction fears.

William Thomson, 1812 - Verses 1 and 2.
Allan J.R. Thomson, 2010 - Verses 3,4 and 5.

Note - Clerkhill Farm, Peterhead, is no longer in existence. The land that it stood on is now covered by a housing estate and Clerkhill Primary School. Reports of farm visitations reproduced by kind permission of Mr. Nigel D. Fairhead, Secretary & Chamberlain, the Company of Merchants of the City of Edinburgh.

THROWE THE BREE

Sadly, many of our old Scots words, descriptions and sayings are fast disappearing. One such phrase is "Throwe the bree." Bree in Scots means water, juice or indeed any liquid. "Barley bree" is whisky for example or "sna' bree" for slush. Any of the juices produced when cooking beef, chicken etc. are also known as bree. To "bree the tatties" is to pour the water off the potatoes when they are boiled. In Scots, if you "let the tatties throwe the bree" it means you have let them boil too long until they have become mushy and spoilt. However, the English words lose something in the translation and do not have the same connotation as "Ye've latten the tatties throwe the bree.

A workin man is nae muckle eass
Fin socht tae help in the hoose
He canna darn a sock that's holed
Nor tichen a button that's loose.

He'll dry the dishes juist fin socht
But that's as far as he goes
An as for cooken he wull resist
Tho' he'll steer a bowl o's brose.

He'd raither sleep in the fireside cheer
Than struggle wi bairnies three
An if left tae watch the tatties bile
He'll lat them throwe the bree.

AULD LANG SYNE

Everyone knows this old Scottish song. It is said that on hearing an old man singing it, Robert Burns re-wrote the words which are the ones we use today. It is sung all over the world on hogmanay, at the end of functions and also on departures. The words that are sung aren't always true to what Burns wrote, nevertheless we should be glad that this song has such wide appeal. Furth of Scotland, the word "Syne" is pronounced "Zyne" which is quite wrong and grates on the ears of those who know the correct pronunciation, i.e. "Sign" as in traffic sign or "Sign" as in sign your name.

Should auld acquaintance be forgot
And never brocht tae min'
So lilts the words o' this auld sang
O' Auld Lang Syne.

It's sung at every place on earth
In puir hames and in fine.
And keeps a place dear in oor hert
The words o' Auld Lang Syne.

It's aye sang late on hogmanay
When bells they start tae chime
An mony a tear is aften shed
When singin' Auld Lang Syne.

We think o' folk that we aince knew
Guid freens o' yours an' mine
Oh happy were the days we spent
In Auld Lang Syne.

But forrit noo we a' should look
An stracht we'll walk the line.
As hand in hand we onward go
Awa' fae Auld Lang Syne.

GLOSSARY OF SCOTTISH WORDS

A	*All*
AAL	*Old*
AALER	*Older*
AALEST	*Oldest*
ABEEN	*Above*
ABOOT	*About*
ACH	*Oh!*
ACHT	*Eight*
ADEE	*To do*
AE	*One*
AFF	*Off*
AFF'I FANG	*Askew/astray*
AFFEN	*Often*
AFORE	*Before*
AFT	*Often/oft*
AICHTY	*Eighty*
AIGGS	*Eggs*
AIN	*Own*
AINCE	*Once*
AIPPLE	*Apple*
AIRM(S)	*Arm(s)*
AIRSE(S)	*Arse(s)*
AITEN	*Eaten*
ALEEN	*Alone*
ALMICHTY	*Almighty*
AM	*I am*
AMON	*Amongst*
ANETH	*Below/under*
ANIDDER	*Another*
ANITHER	*Another*
AROON	*Around*
ASHIMMER	*Shimmering*
AT	*That*
AT A	*At all*
ATE	*Eat*

AULD	*Old*
AVA	*At all*
AWA	*Away*
AYE	*Always*
BAA(S)	*Ball(s)*
BADE	*Lived*
BAGGIE	*Bag/sack*
BAIRNS	*Children*
BAITH	*Both*
BARRA	*Barrow*
BASHFU	*Bashful/shy*
BEEN(S)	*Bone(s)*
BEETS	*Boots*
BELLIES	*Stomachs*
BEN	*Through/along*
BENT	*Sand dune*
BESOMS	*Brooms*
BICKERS	*Large soup plates*
BIDE	*Stay/remain*
BIELD	*Shelter/refuge*
BIGGET	*Built*
BIGGIN	*Building*
BIGSY	*Conceited/self-important*
BILIN/BILT	*Boiling/Boilt*
BIRSE	*Hackles*
BLAA(N)	*Blow(n)*
BLAA(S)	*Blow(s)/boasts*
BLACK AFFRONTED	*Ashamed and embarassed*
BLAKE	*Shoe Polish*
BLEED	*Blood*
BLEEZIN	*Blazing*
BLIN LUMP	*Boil/carbuncle*
BLOO	*Blue*
BLUID	*Blood*
BOABBY	*Police constable*

184

GLOSSARY OF SCOTTISH WORDS

BOCHT	*Bought*
BODDEM	*Bottom*
BOGIE ROLL	*Thick black tobacco*
BOOD	*Bent*
BOOKIE	*Bible*
BOOL	*Marble*
BOO(S)	*Bend(s)*
BOTHY	*Accomodation for single farm worker*
BRAKFIST	*Breakfast*
BRAE(S)	*Hill(s)*
BRA(W)	*Fine/excellent*
BREE	*Water/juice*
BREEKS	*Trousers/knickers*
BREET	*Brute*
BREID	*Bread/or oatcakes*
BRICHT	*Bright*
BRIKS	*Trousers/knickers*
BRITHER	*Brother*
BROB	*Jag*
BROCH	*Fraserburgh*
BROCHT	*Brought*
BROOK	*Soot encrusted*
BROON	*Brown*
BROSE	*Mixture of oatmeal, water, salt & milk*
BROTH	*Scotch broth/thick soup*
BRUISED CORN	*Oats that have been through a bruiser*
BRUNT	*Burnt*
BULLERS	*Hamlet nr. Peterhead "u" pron. as in "Colours"*
BUMMERS	*Factory hooters/Bumble Bees*
BYE	*Past*
BYKE	*Bees nest*
BYRE	*Cow shed*
CA	*Knock*
CA	*Call*
CAAL	*Cold*

GLOSSARY OF SCOTTISH WORDS

CA'ED	*Called*
CAIRRET	*Carried*
CAM	*Came*
CAMES	*Honeycombs*
CANLE	*Candle*
CANNA	*Can't/cannot*
CANNAE	*Careful*
CARVET	*Carved*
CASSEN	*Cast/squint*
CAULD	*Cold*
CHAA	*Chew*
CHAPPET	*Hammered/mashed*
CHATTIE	*Chat/conversation*
CHEER	*Chair*
CHESSEL	*Cheese press*
CHIK	*Cheek/impertinence*
CHIEL	*Chap/fellow*
CHILPIN	*Chittering/cold*
CHINE	*Chain*
CHOCKET	*Chocked*
CHUCKINS	*Chickens/hens*
CHUNTY	*Chamberpot/potty*
CLAA	*Scratch*
CLACHAN	*Hamlet*
CLAES	*Clothes/blankets*
CLAIKEN	*Gossiping*
CLAITH	*Cloth*
CLAP	*Smack*
CLART	*Clort*
CLAS	*Claws*
CLATTIN	*Thinning/hoeing turnips*
CLAW	*Scratch*
CLEEKIT	*Linked arms*
CLIMM'D	*Climbed*
CLIPED	*Told tales on*

GLOSSARY OF SCOTTISH WORDS

CLOODS	*Clouds*
CLOOT	*Cloth*
CLORT	*Smear*
CLORTY	*Wet/dirty*
CLOSS	*Three sided quadrangle of farm buildings*
CLYES	*Clothes*
CONTERMASHIOUS	*Contrary/stubborn*
CO-OPY	*Co-operative Society*
COO	*Cow*
COONCIL	*Council*
COONCILLORS	*Councillors*
COONTED	*Counted*
COORSE	*Bad/severe/wicked*
COORTED(ING)	*Courted/courting*
CORNYARDS	*Stack yards*
CORTER O' BREID	*Oat cake*
COUP	*Rubbish tip*
COUPLES	*Rafters*
COUTHY	*Homely/friendly*
COWKS	*Retches*
COWKEN	*Retching*
CRAALT	*Crawled*
CRABBIT	*Bad tempered*
CRACKET	*Cracked*
CRAFT	*Croft*
CRAFTER	*Crofter*
CRAP	*Crop*
CWYLES	*Coals*
CWYTES	*Coates*
DAAD	*Piece*
DAE	*Do*
DAMPT	*Damned*
DAR	*Dare*
DEE	*Do/die*
DEEF	*Deaf*

GLOSSARY OF SCOTTISH WORDS

DEEM	*Woman*
DEEN	*Done*
DEEIN	*Doing/dying*
DEID	*Dead*
DEID THRAA	*Stubborn huff/sulk*
DEILS	*Devils*
DENNIR	*Dinner*
DEUK	*Duck*
DICHT(ED)	*Wipe(ed)*
DILSE	*Dulse/seaweed*
DIRDIN	*Bouncing/jarring*
DIRL	*Hurt/vibrate with pain*
DIV	*Do*
DIVVY	*Dividend*
DIZZEN	*Dozen*
DOCKS	*Bums/bottoms*
DOMINIE	*Headmaster*
DOON	*Down*
DOOT	*Doubt*
DOTHER(S)	*Daughter(s)*
DRAARS	*Drawers/underpants*
DREEL(S)	*Drill(s)*
DREEPS	*Drips*
DREICH	*Wet, cold and miserable*
DRIBBLES	*Wet weather*
DROON	*Drown*
DROOTH	*Thirst*
DRYSTANE	*Dry stone*
DUBBY	*Muddy*
DUG	*Dog*
DUTCHES	*Ditches*
DYKE	*Wall*
'EAR	*Year*
EASS	*Use*
EASED	*Used to*

GLOSSARY OF SCOTTISH WORDS

EE	*The/In the/To the*
E'E	*Eye*
EEN	*Eyes or one*
EENCE	*Once*
EENS	*Ones*
EERAN'S	*Errands/messages/groceries*
EFTER	*After*
EFTERNEEN	*Afternoon*
ENEUCH	*Enough*
ERE	*There*
ESTREEN	*Yesterday*
FADDER	*Father*
FA	*Who*
FAA OOT	*Fall out*
FAAR	*Far*
FAARER	*Further*
FAA(S)	*Who/who is*
FAE	*From*
FACTOR	*Landowner's agent*
FAIRM	*Farm*
FAIRM TOUN	*Farm steading*
FAN	*When*
FARFAR	*Forfar*
FAR(S)	*Where(s)*
FART	*Flatulate*
FEART	*Frightened*
FEE'D	*Contracted to work*
FEEL	*Fool*
FEMILY	*Family*
FILE(S)	*While(s)*
FIN	*When/find*
FIT(S)	*Foot/what(s)*
FIT LIKE	*How are you*
FITE	*White*
FITIVVER	*Whatever*

GLOSSARY OF SCOTTISH WORDS

FLAIR	*Floor*
FLEE	*Fly*
FLEEIN	*Flying*
FLEER	*Floor*
FLICHT	*Flight*
FOO	*Why/how*
FLOOERS	*Flowers*
FORRIT	*Forward*
FOWER	*Four*
FOWK	*Folk*
FREEN	*Friend*
FRICHTENED	*Frightened*
FU	*Full*
FULE	*Dirty/foul*
FUN	*Found*
FUNCY	*Fancy*
FUNS	*Whins/gorse*
FUSKIE	*Whisky*
FUSSLE	*Whistle*
GAAN	*Going*
GAE	*Go*
GAED	*Went*
GAEN	*Gone*
GAIRDEN	*Garden*
GAITHERED	*Gathered*
GALLUSSES	*Braces*
GANE	*Gone*
GANG	*Go*
GARR(S)	*Make(s)*
GARRT	*Made*
GEEIN	*Giving*
GEEN	*Gone*
GEETS	*Children*
GIE	*Very*
GIN	*Come/if*

GLOSSARY OF SCOTTISH WORDS

GING	*Go*
GIRN	*Moan/complain*
GIRNAL	*Wooden cabinet for storing oatmeal*
GLESS	*Glass*
GLESSES	*Glasses/spectacles*
GLOWER	*Stare*
GOAD	*God*
GOLLACH	*Beatle*
GOOSSERS	*Gooseberries*
GOWDEN	*Golden*
GOWKS	*Fools*
GOWPEN FU	*Double cupped handful*
GRALLOCH	*Deer offal*
GRAN	*Grand*
GREENIE POLES	*Clothes poles*
GREET	*Cry/sob*
GRUN	*Ground*
GRUNNY	*Grandmother*
GUID	*Good*
GUIDWIFE	*Mistress of the house*
GWEED	*Good*
GYAD SAKES	*God sakes*
GYANG(S)	*Go(es)*
GYLIES	*Often/very*
HACKER	*Hawker/Pedlar*
HACKET	*Covered in chaps*
HACKIN	*Barking*
HADNAE	*Hadn't*
HAE	*Have*
HALE	*Whole*
HALF A CROON	*Half a Crown - 2 shillings & sixpence (22 1/2 p)*
HAME	*Home*
HAMELY	*Homely*
HAN	*Hand*
HANLT	*Handled*

GLOSSARY OF SCOTTISH WORDS

HAUL	*Pull*
HEDDER	*Heather*
HEICH(EST)	*High(est)*
HEID	*Head*
HEILAN	*Highland*
HEMMERT	*Hammered*
HENNY'S	*Hen/Chicken(s)*
HERT	*Heart*
HET	*Hot*
HETTER	*Hotter*
HEUGHS	*Cliffs*
HICHT	*Height*
HID	*Had/hidden*
HIDIN	*Leathering/chastisement*
HINE	*Very far*
HING	*Hang*
HINGIN	*Hanging*
HINMAIST	*Hindmost/last*
HINNA	*Have not*
HINNERAIN	*At the end of the day*
HIPPENS	*Nappies*
HIV	*Have*
HOAST	*Cough*
HOGMANAY	*New Year's Eve*
HOOSE	*House*
HOTTERIN	*Simmering*
HOW	*Hoe*
HOWE	*Valley*
HOWKET	*Dug*
HUD	*Hold*
HUDDLET	*Huddled*
HUFF	*Sulks*
HULLS	*Hills*
HULT	*Halt*
HUMPHY	*Hunchback*

GLOSSARY OF SCOTTISH WORDS

HUNKIE	*Handkerchief*
HUNDER	*Hundred*
HUNNER	*Hundred*
HURRIET	*Hurried*
HYE	*Hay*
I	*The*
IDDER	*Other*
ILE	*Oil*
ILKY	*Every*
ILL TRICKET	*Full of devilment*
ILL WULL	*Grudge/dislike*
IMSEL	*Himself*
INGANS	*Onions*
INNA	*As well*
ISNAE	*Is not/isn't*
ISS	*This*
ITHER(S)	*Other(s)*
IV NOO	*Just now*
IVVER	*Ever*
JALOUSED	*Suspected/guessed*
JAUNTY	*Self confident/big headed*
JILE	*Jail*
JINED	*Joined*
JINER	*Joiner*
JIST/JUIST	*Just*
KAIMED	*Combed*
KEN(S)	*Know(s)*
KENT	*Knew/known*
KINE(S)	*Kind(s)*
KINT	*Knew*
KIS	*Because*
KIST	*Chest made of pine*
KITTLINS	*Kittens*
KITCHIE DEEM	*Kitchen maid/ domestic servant*
KYE	*Cattle*

GLOSSARY OF SCOTTISH WORDS

LAA	*Law*
LAAVIE	*Toilet*
LACH	*Laugh*
LACHED	*Laughed*
LACHIN	*Laughing*
LACHTER	*Laughter*
LAFT	*Loft*
LAICH	*Low lying lands*
LAIRD	*Lord/land owner*
LANG	*Long*
LANGER	*Longer*
LANG SEEN	*Long ago*
LARRY	*Lorry*
LASTIC	*Elastic*
LAT	*Let*
LAVE	*Remains/what was left over*
LEDDER	*Leather/beat*
LEDDERT	*Leathered/beaten*
LEES	*Lies*
LEST	*Last*
LICHT	*Light*
LICHTER	*Lighter*
LICHTSOME	*Lightsome*
LICKY	*Spot/small amount*
LILTS	*Swings*
LINGTH	*Length*
LOABBY	*Lobby/hall*
LOOD	*Loud*
LOON	*Boy/lad*
LOUP	*Jump/leap*
LOUSED	*Stopped work*
LUDGINS	*Lodgings*
LUGS	*Ears*
LUM	*Chimney*
LUMP(S)	*Lamp(s)*

GLOSSARY OF SCOTTISH WORDS

MA	*Me*
MALEEN	*Alone*
MAIR	*More*
MAIRRIET	*Married*
MAIST	*Most*
MAISTLY	*Mostly*
MAIT TIME	*Meal times*
MAK	*Make*
MAK'S	*Makes*
MAM	*Mum/mother*
MANNIE	*Man*
MANNIES	*Men*
MARKET	*Marked*
MARRA	*Marrowfat*
MASEL	*Myself*
MAUN	*Must*
MEAL	*Oat meal*
MEALIE DUMPLIN	*Dumpling of oatmeal, suet & onions*
MEALIE JIMMIES	*White puddings*
MEEN	*Moon*
MEENIT	*Minute*
MEENLICHT	*Moonlight*
MEENTY	*Minute*
METTER	*Matter*
MICHTY	*Mighty*
MIDDER	*Mother*
MILT	*Melt*
MIN	*Man*
MINE	*Mind/remember*
MISSIN	*Missing*
MITH	*Might*
MITHER	*Mother*
MITHER'S	*Mother's*
MOCHIE	*Humid and damp*
MONY	*Many*

GLOSSARY OF SCOTTISH WORDS

MOO	*Mouth*
MORN	*Tomorrow*
MOSS	*Muirland where pits are dug out*
MUCK	*Dung/manure*
MUCKLE	*Big/large or Much*
MULL	*Mill*
MULLART	*Miller*
MYE	*May*
NAE	*No/Not*
NAETHING	*Nothing*
NARRA	*Narrow*
NEEBOURS	*Neighbours*
NEEN	*None*
NEEP(S)	*Turnip(s)*
NEIST	*Next*
NEUK	*Corner*
NICHT	*Night*
NIVVER	*Never*
NOO	*Now*
O	*Of*
ONY	*Any*
ONYWYE	*Anyway*
OOR	*Our/hour*
OORSEL'S	*Ourselves*
OOT	*Out*
O'T	*Of it*
OWER	*Over*
PAIRINS	*Peelings*
PANLOAF	*Posh affected speech*
PARKS	*Fields*
PARTEECLAR	*Particular*
PECHS	*Sighs/gasps*
PEELS	*Pills*
PEER	*Poor*
PEY	*Pay*

GLOSSARY OF SCOTTISH WORDS

PIDDLET	*Peed*
PINT	*Point*
PINTS	*Laces*
PISE	*Peas*
PISHIN	*Pissing/pouring*
PIT	*Put*
PITTEN	*Putting*
PLAISED	*Pleased*
PLETTIE	*Platform/Veranda*
PLOO	*Plough*
PLOOKY	*Pimply*
PLUNKET	*Plopped/dropped*
POOCHES	*Pockets*
POODERS	*Powders*
POOR	*Pour*
PORRITCH	*Porridge*
PREEN	*Pin*
PRESS	*Cupboard*
PROOD	*Proud*
PU(D)	*Pull(ed)*
PUCKLE	*Several*
PUCKLIE	*Small amount*
PUDDOCK	*Frog*
PUIR	*Poor*
PUN(S)	*Pound(s)*
PUSS	*Face*
PYOKE	*Bag/jute sack*
QUATE	*Quiet*
QUATENED	*Quietened*
QUINE(S)	*Girl(s)*
QUIZZEN	*Questioning/asking*
QWEELS	*Cools/chills*
RAA	*Raw/Row*
RAAS	*Rows*
RAIKET	*Searched/raked*

RAIVELLET	*Untidy/mixed up*
RAKED	*Searched*
RARE	*Good/excellent*
RAX	*Stretch*
REEF	*Roof*
REEKY	*Smoky*
REEKET	*Reeked*
REID	*Red*
RIGGET OOT	*Rigged out*
RIGGIN	*Middle*
RICHT(S)	*Right(s)*
RIK	*Smoke/reek*
RIFT	*Belch*
RIN	*Run*
ROADIES	*Small twisted paths*
ROCH	*Rough*
RODDEN	*Rowan*
ROON	*Round*
ROOSTIN	*Rusting*
ROUP	*Auction sale*
ROWIES	*Rolls*
RUBBIT	*Rabbit*
SA	*Saw*
SAAT(Y)	*Salt(y)*
SAFT	*Soft*
SAIR	*Sore*
SAN	*Sand*
SARKS	*Shirts*
SASSAGES	*Sausages*
SAX	*Six*
SCINT	*Scent*
SCOTCH	*Scottish*
SCRANY	*Scrawny*
SCRATCHET	*Scratched*
SECKIT	*Put in a sack*

GLOSSARY OF SCOTTISH WORDS

SEEMIT	*Vest*
SEEN	*Since/soon*
SEEVEN	*Seven*
SEYVIN	*Seven*
SEL	*Self*
SELLT	*Sold*
SHAAS	*Shaws*
SHAIR	*Sure*
SHAK	*Shake*
SHAKKIN	*Shaking*
SHAKKIN(S)	*Dross/remnants*
SHEEN	*Shoes*
SHEWIN	*Sewing*
SHILLIN	*Shilling - 5 pence*
SHOD	*Put shoes on*
SHOOERY	*Showery*
SHUID	*Should*
SHUNNERS	*Cinders*
SIC	*Such*
SIC	*Sixpence (2 ¹/₂ pence)*
SICHT	*Sight*
SICKEN	*Seeking/wanting*
SILLER	*Silver/money/cash*
SIMMER	*Summer*
SITTY	*Sooty*
SKELPIT	*Spanked/smacked*
SKIRLIE	*Oatmeal seasoned & fried in a pot with chopped onion*
SKIRL	*Squeal*
SKIRLIN	*Squealing*
SKWEEL	*School*
SLIDDER	*Slippery icy conditions*
SMIDDY	*Smithy*
SMORE	*Smother - as in smothering, drifing snow*
SNA	*Snow*

GLOSSARY OF SCOTTISH WORDS

SNAVVIE	*Snowy*
SNAVVIE BREE	*Snowy melt water*
SNOD	*Tidy*
SNUFFIN	*Sniffing*
SOAKEN	*Soaking*
SOCHT	*Sought/asked*
SONSIE	*Well built/plump*
SOOK	*Suck*
SOOND(ED)	*Sound(ed)*
SOOR	*Sour*
SOOROCK	*Wood Sorrel*
SOOTH	*South*
SOSHIE	*Co-operative*
SOUGH(ED)	*Sigh(ed)*
SOUGHEN	*Sighing*
SOUN	*Sound*
SPEENS	*Spoons*
SPEIR	*Ask*
SPEWIN	*Vomiting*
SPICE	*Pepper*
SPIK(S)	*Speak(s)*
SPIKKEN	*Speaking*
SPILE	*Spoil*
SPILT	*Spoilt*
SPLYOCHAN	*Tobacco pouch*
SPOOT	*Rain gutter*
SPUE	*Vomit*
SPUNK(S)	*Match(es)*
STAMMACK	*Stomach*
STANE(S)/STEEN(S)	*Stone(s)*
STANNIN	*Standing*
STAN'S	*Stands*
STAPPIT	*Stuffed/blocked*
STEED	*Stood*
STEEN(Y)(S)	*Stone(y)(s)/14 lbs weight*

GLOSSARY OF SCOTTISH WORDS

STEER	*Stir/ a hasty muddle*
STEMS	*Potato shaws*
STIBBLES	*Stubbles*
STIRK	*Young cattle beast*
STOOKIE	*Plaster*
STOOKS	*Sheaves of grain set out in a field to dry*
STOOR	*Dust*
STOOT	*Stout*
STOTTET	*Bounced*
STOVIES	*Potatoes, onions & diced beef fried*
STRACHT	*Straight*
STRAPPIN	*Muscular/well built*
STROOP	*Spout*
STUMPET	*Stamped*
STUNNIN'	*Standing*
SULKET	*Sulked*
SUNBRUNT	*Sunburnt*
SUP	*Some/a drop*
SURLY	*Dour/bad tempered*
SWALLED	*Swelled*
SWANKS	*Struts/swaggers*
SWEDDISH	*Swede*
SWEEL	*Rinse*
SWICK	*Cheat*
SWIER	*Swear*
SWIERT	*Reluctant/loathe*
SWITE	*Sweat*
SYNE	*Then*
TAE	*To*
TAED	*Toed*
TAEN	*Taken*
TAES	*Toes*
TAG	*Belt/tawse*
TAK	*Take*
TAP	*Top*

GLOSSARY OF SCOTTISH WORDS

TATTIE	*Potato*
TAY	*Tea*
TEE	*Too/also/to the*
TEEM(T)	*Empty/emptied*
TEEN	*Took/taken*
TELLT	*Told*
THAA	*Thaw*
THAE	*Those*
THEGIDDER	*Altogether/together*
THEGITHER	*Together*
THERMAGENE	*Orange cotton wool type fabric worn under the vest*
THOCHT	*Thought*
THOLE	*Bear*
THOOM	*Thumb*
THRAAN	*Awkward/ill tempered*
THRAWIN	*Awkward/ill tempered*
THREID	*Thread*
THROWE	*Through*
THRUMS	*Kirriemuir*
TIBACCA	*Tobacco*
TICHEN	*Tighten*
TICHT	*Tight*
TIG	*Huff/sulks*
TINKS	*Tinkers/travelling people*
TODDIES	*Whisky & hot water*
TOON	*Town*
TOONSER	*Townsmen*
TRACHLED	*Wearily struggling*
TRAIVELLET	*Travelled*
TRUMP	*Stand on/tread*
TUGGY	*Tousled/knotted*
TULL	*To*
TULLS	*To us/me*
TUMMEL	*Tumble*
TURRA	*Turriff*

GLOSSARY OF SCOTTISH WORDS

TWA	*Two*
TWAL	*Twelve*
TWATHREE	*Two or three*
TYANGS	*Tongs*
TYKE	*Mongrel dog*
ULL FASHIONED	*Nosey*
UMMAN	*Woman as a term of endearment*
UNCE	*Ounce*
UNCO	*Very*
UPTAK	*Uptake/contact*
VAUNTY	*Proud*
VICE	*Voice*
VRATCH	*Wretch*
VROCHT	*Worked*
WA(S)	*Wall(s)*
WAAK	*Walk*
WAAL	*Well*
WAALDIES	*Wellingtons*
WAISCUIT	*Waistcoat*
WAALL	*Well*
WAAN	*Wand/stick*
WALLY	*China*
WANTIN	*Without*
WATTER	*Water*
WAUR	*Worse*
WEEDA	*Widow*
WEEL	*Well*
WEER	*Wear*
WEET	*Wet*
WERRLISS	*Wireless/radio*
WHAUR	*Where*
WHEATSTRAE	*Wheat straw*
WHEELVRICHT	*Wheelright*
WHILIE	*While*
WI	*With*

GLOSSARY OF SCOTTISH WORDS

WIK	*Week*
WID	*Would*
WIDDEN	*Wooden*
WIDDER	*Weather*
WIMES	*Stomachs/bellies*
WINDAE	*Window*
WINNER	*Wonder*
WINN'S	*Winds*
WINN'Y	*Windy*
WIR	*Our*
WIRD	*Word*
WIRSELS	*Ourselves*
WIS	*Was*
WISNA	*Wasn't*
WITE	*Wait*
WITIN	*Waiting*
WITHER	*Weather*
WITHERED	*Weathered*
WORSIT	*Woollen*
WRACKET	*Wracked*
WRANG	*Wrong*
WREATHS	*Snow drifts*
WUID	*Wood*
WULL	*Will*
WUMMAN	*Woman*
WUNNA	*Won't/will not*
WYE	*Way*
WYED	*Weighed*
YAISED	*Used*
YALLA	*Yellow*
YE	*You*
YELLA	*Yellow*
YOAMIN	*Billowing*
YOKET	*Yoked/started*
YOWE(S)	*Ewe/Ewes*